WHEN THE *MARRIED* PERSON BECOMES THE *MISTRESS*

Unbreakable Bonds

CONTENTS

INTRODUCTION

The power of unity, both in the physical and spiritual realms, is immeasurable. It forms the foundation for oneness, fostering growth and progress in all aspects of our lives. This intimacy in our relationships with God and our spouses is precisely what the devil strives to disrupt. His aim is to sever these bonds and lead us astray.

To achieve this, he employs a myriad of strategies, both spiritual and otherwise, to execute his plans. Often, believers—his primary targets—remain unaware of his schemes. Consequently, many fall prey to his deceptive tactics.

This book is written to equip believers with biblical knowledge, enabling them not just to resist becoming estranged but also to overcome the guilt, shame, and depression that may follow. It is structured into five interconnected chapters, each presented in a clear and comprehensible manner.

Don't just get a copy for yourself; share it with anyone seeking to restore their intimacy with God and their partner to its original state. See you at the top!.

CHAPTER ONE

THE POWER OF DECISION

I have a pattern of thinking whenever I come across people that are in a bad condition or state of their lives. Usually, my thought in such situations is that the concerned persons were once occupied with positive thinking, dreams, and aspirations on how to better and improve their lives. These individuals likely envisioned a bright future, filled with success and happiness. However, these people made some bad decisions that brought them to where they are currently. They literally allowed themselves to become influenced by wrong associations, poor choices, and other negative behaviors.

As a result of these decisions, they are now walking down a dark path in their lives, a path shaped by their own very unwise decisions. Ordinarily, this is a place or condition that they never could have imagined finding themselves in. It's a stark contrast to the hopeful and ambitious dreams they once had, an unexpected and often painful reality.

The bad decisions of these people make them settle for less in the affairs of life, instead of reaching out for the best or top position that they had always dreamed of attaining. Automatically, they begin to experience all-around changes in their lives. This change is typically characterized by a comparison between where they used to be and where they are currently. The differences in these two positions normally inject feelings of unworthiness and regret into their psyches.

It's heartbreaking to witness the transformation as these once hopeful individuals grapple with the consequences of their actions. They might lose confidence in their abilities, become hesitant to take new opportunities, or even fall into a state of despair. The weight of their unwise choices hangs heavily over them, altering their outlook on life and diminishing their inner drive.

The journey from hope to regret is a poignant reminder of how crucial our decisions are in shaping our lives. It underscores the importance of surrounding ourselves with positive influences and making thoughtful, considered choices. Yet, even in this bleak scenario, there's always a glimmer of hope - the potential for redemption and the possibility of a second chance to redirect their lives onto a more positive path. Recognizing the depth of their situation can be the first step towards rebuilding and striving again for those once cherished dreams.

In the end, it's not about avoiding mistakes altogether, but how we learn from them and move forward. It's about holding onto hope and never giving up on ourselves, no matter how challenging the road may seem. And with perseverance and determination, even those who have fallen from great heights can rise again to achieve their true potential. Let this be a lesson to us all - that our decisions truly hold the power to shape our destinies and ultimately determine the course of our lives. So let us choose wisely and dream big, knowing that anything is possible if we are willing to put in the effort and make wise choices along the way. Let us never lose sight of our dreams and aspirations, for they are what drive us to be the best version of ourselves and reach our full potential. The journey may not always be easy, but it will always be worth it in the end. So let us strive to make every decision count, knowing that each one has the power to shape our future and lead us towards a life filled with purpose, fulfillment, and happiness. As we navigate through life's ups and downs, let us remember that our choices matter and have the ability to define who we are as individuals. And in the face of any setbacks or failures, let us always hold onto hope and belief in ourselves, for it is never too late to turn our lives around and create a brighter future. So let us embrace the potential of second chances and continue to dream big, live with passion, and make each day count towards a life well-lived.

As we reflect on the power of making choices, it's important to also recognize the impact that our actions have on those around us. The decisions we make not only affect our own lives but also those of our loved ones, friends, and even strangers we encounter along the way. Our actions can inspire others to reach for their own dreams and make positive changes in their lives. So let us use our choices to not only better ourselves but also to uplift and empower those around us.

Furthermore, it's important to remember that we are constantly evolving and growing as individuals. As we continue on our journey towards our dreams, we may find that our goals and desires change along the way. And that's okay. It's all part of the process of discovering who we are and what truly makes us happy. So let us be open to new opportunities, embrace change, and never be afraid to pursue a different path if it leads us towards greater fulfillment and happiness.

In conclusion, let us never underestimate the power of our choices. They have the ability to shape our present and future, impact those around us, and ultimately determine our overall level of happiness and satisfaction in life. So let us make each choice with intention, purpose, and the belief that we are capable of creating a life filled with purpose and meaning. Let us embrace the journey towards self-discovery and continue to make choices that align with who we truly are. Live boldly, dream big, and create a life that brings you joy and fulfillment every day. So keep making those choices wisely as they will ultimately define who we are and the legacy we leave behind. Let us choose to live our lives with intention, purpose, and passion, and inspire others to do the same. So go out there, embrace your power of choice, and create a life that you are proud of. The possibilities are endless when we realize the impact our choices have on ourselves and the world around us. So let's make them count! Keep dreaming big and never stop taking action towards making your dreams a reality. You have the power to shape your own destiny - so use it wisely and purposefully. With each choice you make, remember that you are shaping your life and the person you become. So choose to be brave, choose to be kind, choose to be true to yourself, and watch as your choices lead you towards a life of purpose, joy, and fulfillment. Embrace the power of choice and live your best life today! .

Listen to this: as long as the person involved continues to play the role of the side chick, it becomes much more difficult for them to come out of it because of the depression, guilt, shame, and other negative emotions associated with it. Over time, these feelings can become overwhelming, creating a psychological trap that makes escape seem nearly impossible. Most times, they choose to remain and even die in it rather than coming out, believing that they're trapped in a cycle that they cannot break free from.

Maybe as a mistress, you are currently experiencing the same change of roles from headship to internship in every dimension of your life. As a result, your life is now in a wreck, and you are contemplating what to do to regain your freedom. You may find yourself feeling isolated and desperate, unsure of where to turn for help. I have good news for you: you are not the only one in this bad condition of life. There are millions of people out there who are going through the same ugly experience just like you, feeling trapped and alone.

My sincere desire is to bring you help, not just on how to avoid becoming a mistress, but to also help those of you who are already one to overcome your guilt, shame, and regrets. I want to guide you to embrace realities that would lead you to return to your former roles. This desire to provide support and guidance is what inspired and motivated me to write this book. I understand the emotional turmoil you may be going through, and I want to offer you practical advice and encouragement.

Now, there are people who have this tough and not-easy-to-change mentality on how they do things, even in their marriages and relationships. They may have grown up in environments where unhealthy behaviors were normalized, and as a result, they carry those patterns into their adult lives. Most times, you discover that these people behave this way as a result of the bad treatment and emotional hurt that they received from their parents who mentored them. These early experiences can have a profound impact on how they interact with others and manage their relationships.

If these people desire their freedom, the only solution available to them is to seek out and submit to a mentor who can help them to overcome their bitterness. This mentor can offer a new perspective and support them in making positive changes. Except this is done, they would continue to make wrong decisions with disastrous mistakes based on the bitterness in their hearts. It's a difficult journey, but one that is essential for breaking free from the cycle of pain and poor choices.

It's also very important that in the reality of the changing world that we are in today, we should endeavor to correct how we were trained and what was negatively passed down to us. This attitude would help us to reduce the high possibilities of us moving from the position of being married to that of the mistress. By recognizing and addressing these inherited behaviors, we can create healthier relationships and avoid repeating the mistakes of the past.

The extent to which we are able to align or stoop to these positive changes in our relationships determines the level of matrimonial bond and happiness that we are to enjoy in it. Have you ever asked yourself this important question, "What do I have to stoop to, just to make my marriage better and stronger?" Being willing to make these changes can lead to a more fulfilling and stable relationship.

I know of a man who was a street lord, a womanizer, and a drug dealer. This dude was always in the clubhouse every weekend with his crew, living a life of recklessness and danger. I once had an encounter with him where he attempted to shoot me using his gun, in a basement after a party. He asked a friend of mine to tell me something bad about my mother so that I would react, and then, he would jealously shoot me. But as God may have it, I didn't react as he thought that I would. After his demise, I came to discover more about his life and the struggles he faced. His story is a reminder of the importance of seeking help and making positive changes before it's too late. If we want to break the cycle of negative behaviors and attitudes in our relationships, we must be willing to face our past and make necessary changes for a better future.

In conclusion, it is essential for us to understand that our behavior and attitude in relationships are influenced by our upbringing and environment. However, it is never too late to make positive changes and break free from inherited toxic patterns. By recognizing these influences and taking proactive steps towards healthier habits, we can cultivate stronger, happier, and more fulfilling relationships. Let us always strive to create an atmosphere of love, trust, respect, and understanding in all our relationships. Together, we can break the cycle and build a better future for ourselves and our loved ones. So let's be willing to take responsibility, seek help, and make necessary changes for the sake of healthy and happy relationships. Let us never forget that change starts with us.

Throughout their marriage, she remained steadfast in her faith and commitment, even when faced with numerous challenges and heartaches. She prayed for strength and guidance, hoping that things would improve.

I am not in any way at all trying to condemn this man on how he lived his life. However, my sole concern and interest were on his wife, and all the pains she had to endure in the hands of this man, just to avoid being a mistress. Many women in her position have had to divorce their husbands many times, thinking they would find another man that's much better. They keep jumping from one relationship to another, often believing that the next partner will provide the happiness and stability they seek.

Some of them would even reason that after their divorces, they would get that man of their dream that would treat them well. "But do you know what?" Such dreams of theirs never saw the light of the day. As a result, they didn't have any other option other than to remain in the position of the mistress. They find themselves in a cycle of broken relationships and unmet expectations, each experience leaving them more disillusioned.

This woman in question must have discovered that she had made the mistake that many other women do make, which is marrying the wrong person. However, she decided to deal with it, instead of seeking a divorce. She chose to stay married rather than become a mistress. What a bold decision! Her choice was not just about enduring hardship but about finding a way to make her marriage work despite the odds.

I know you might be prompted to condemn her decision, but you don't have to do so. After all, different women have different approaches as well as strategies on how they handle their marital issues, and the strategies that work for them. If the woman had failed to work out her marriage, the implication is that she would have remained a side chick.

These side chicks or mistresses go through a lot of pains, just thinking and comparing where they were before with their present situation. The differences in these two positions normally inject a lot of heartache, cries, depression, and regrets into them. They often feel a sense of loss and regret, constantly questioning their past decisions.

I also heard about the story of a woman who was seriously abused by her own husband. This man would always like to pour hot on his wife. However, this woman was endowed more with the grace of endurance and she bore the husband's excesses, just to ensure that her marriage works out. This attitude of the woman made her husband surrender his life to her Jesus. Her unwavering faith and patience eventually led to a transformation in her husband, bringing about a positive change in their relationship.

I want you to know this: it's what we are willing to go through and survive in our hard times that refines our attitude and makes us better in our marriages. But it requires wisdom for us to discern this and follow suit because it's not usually so easy and comfortable. Enduring hardship can build character and resilience, but it takes wisdom to know when to persist and when to seek help.

There are many mistakes that we make in our marriages, just because we don't want to entertain any nonsense from our partner. This attitude has never helped anyone. A lot of women who were previously married are now mistresses because of their intolerable attitude. These women had everything going well for them in their marriages but lacked wisdom, which is the principal thing in the sustenance of a lasting relationship or marriage.

Some of these side chick's women are out of their marriages because of something they would have separately gone to an experienced marriage counselor to get some guidelines for a short period of time. But instead of doing so, they decided to jump out of their marriages in anger, pride, and frustration. Now, they are going through the shameful and rigorous experiences of divorce. They often feel regret, realizing that they could have addressed their issues with professional help.

Some of them thought that if they jump out of the relationship, they will get into a better one. But to their greatest surprises, things didn't just work out the way they had planned. Now, they are trying to work out a relationship with any man. Many have come to understand that finding a perfect partner is not as easy as they once believed.

Many of them are now willing to come back to their husbands and to do what they should have done before they became the mistresses. But the problem here is that these men have now opened their hearts to other women with whom they are currently married. Their former husbands have moved on, finding happiness and stability with new partners.

This is the entitlement of the first wife who was not willing to work out the differences between her and her former husband. They had all the rights and privileges to demand whatsoever they liked from their husband, and it would be met. But now, such rights and privileges have been taken away from them and given to someone else. Now, she has to put up with or bear more things, much more than she used to do before. This is simply because they have gone from the position of being married to that of becoming a mistress.

Many people are in this position of life today. Many started on the right side of being married but are now settling on the wrong side of being mistresses. They find themselves trapped in a cycle of regret and longing for what once was. Don't be one of them!.

CHAPTER TWO

THERE IS HOPE FOR THE MISTRESS

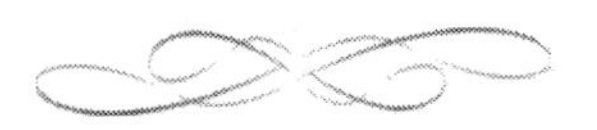

My sincere word to every side chick, who was once married, is that you might get the chance to do it over again. But ensure you get it rightly this second time. Remember, life often grants second chances, but it is up to us to make the most out of them. You must be prepared to learn from past mistakes and grow from those experiences.

However, you must realize as a matter of fact that we live in a fast-changing world. The knowledge of this would help you to navigate through the madness called "life." Adaptability and awareness are key virtues in today's dynamic environment. You need to know first and foremost that the single or unmarried friend of yours, who you hung out with during your singlehood period, isn't the right person for you to take your marital problems to for guidance and counseling. Apparently, they know absolutely nothing about being in a legitimate marriage or relationship, and as such, they can't give you the needed counsel.

Before you even arrive at the decision to consult any of them, you need to have counted the cost of how long you and your spouse have been together; the pains and challenges that the two of you had to bear, among other things, only for you to relinquish your marriage after a short period of time. Reflect on the shared memories, the joys and sorrows, and the mutual growth you have experienced. You see, once you are married, necessity demands that you need to change your singlehood mentality. You can't expect to make meaningful progress in your relationship or marriage while still holding on to unmarried people's mentality. It doesn't work out that way! This behavior has made a lot of married people become mistresses.

These single friends of yours can only give you bitter and misleading counsel that would lead to the crashing of your marriage. The reason being that some of them, especially the female folks, are also interested in marrying your husband and taking your position. So, all their counsel do majorly proceed from a heart of jealousy and envy. Their advice may seem well-intentioned, but underlying motives can distort their guidance.

I want you to know this: the thought of the pains, disrespect, and shame that a wife who wants to go back to her former husband encounters is enough to make you strive to get the right counsel from the right person. You don't have to go through the same ugly experience of emotional and physical hurts that most of them are going through before you would learn to make your marriage work. Learn from the mistakes of others to save yourself from unnecessary heartache. But in all, there's still hope for you because the purpose of this book is to bring you help and encouragement, and to take you from where you are now to where you are meant to be in life.

But the first step to getting help is for you to acknowledge that you made a costly mistake, just like your husband did. After that, you need to realize that you are facing or dealing with what is called, "Soul tie." You might be prompted at this juncture to ask the question, "What is Soul tie?" It is a time when the soul of each person in a relationship is locked towards the other person and needs to be freed. In such situations, you really need to muster the courage and strength to freely walk away because you would be doing yourself much good by doing so.

During this time, you have to reject the man that won't allow you to go because he may have so many things against you in his heart, and at the same time, making it difficult for you to leave. This is a complex and emotionally draining situation, but one that requires you to think clearly and act decisively. At this juncture of your life, you must think about yourself first and how you can move forward. You staying back in such a relationship is like staying back on a vehicle that is heading to nowhere.

Your side chick feeling and emotion is also another thing that you must strongly reject and move on with your life because the man has done so with his own life. You have to keep walking away without giving him the choice to be the one to leave you. It might not be easy, but that's the best thing for you to do!

When a man who has been on drugs for some time wants to withdraw, he would begin to feel empty and unstableness in his mind and body. This might not be so comfortable for him at the initial stage, but it would surely be for his own good in the long run. That's how it is in a relationship when you decide to leave because the mind of your husband has been locked against you.

This is a major reason you should get yourself separated from the people that have the side chick mentality, and cling to strong people for help. Hanging out with people of the same side chick mentality would just continue to make you more depressed. You must be vulnerable and hope to get help because pride could stop your help. Seek out those who have navigated similar paths and emerged stronger, their experiences can be a beacon of hope and guidance for you. Surround yourself with positive and supportive individuals who can help you through this tough time.

Additionally, focus on self-care and self-love. Take care of your physical, emotional and mental well-being. Engage in activities that bring you joy and make you feel good about yourself. This will boost your confidence and remind you of your worth outside of the relationship. It's important to remember that leaving a toxic relationship is not a failure, it's an act of courage and self-love.

Lastly, be patient with yourself. Healing takes time and it won't happen overnight. Allow yourself to feel all the emotions that come with leaving a toxic relationship and work through them. Seek professional help if needed, there is no shame in getting therapy to help you heal and move forward. Remember that you deserve happiness and a healthy relationship, and by leaving the toxic one, you are taking the first step towards achieving that.

In conclusion, leaving a toxic relationship can be difficult but it's necessary for your well-being and mental health. Surround yourself with positive and supportive people, focus on self-care and be patient with yourself during the healing process. Remember that you are not alone and there is always hope for a brighter future. Stay strong and never settle for less than what you deserve. So, keep moving forward and never look back. You are capable of so much more and you deserve to be happy. As the saying goes, "You can't start the next chapter of your life if you keep re-reading the last one." Embrace a new beginning and let go of toxic relationships that hold you back from reaching your full potential. The future is in your hands and it's up to you to make it a bright and healthy one.

So, take care of yourself, seek help when needed, and know that leaving a toxic relationship is an act of courage and self-love. You deserve to be in a loving and respectful relationship, and by leaving the toxic one, you are creating space for that to happen. Trust your instincts and always prioritize your well-being above others' opinions or societal pressures. Remember that leaving a toxic relationship is not giving up, it's taking back control of your life and choosing what's best for you.

In the end, remember that you are strong and capable of overcoming any challenges that come your way. Leaving a toxic relationship may be difficult, but it will lead you towards a healthier and happier future. Trust yourself and have faith that better things are waiting for you on the other side. You are worthy of love, respect, and happiness in all aspects of your life. So, don't be afraid to let go and start a new chapter filled with positivity and self-love. Remember that you have the power to create your own happy ending. Keep moving forward and never settle for anything less than what you deserve. The journey towards healing may not be easy, but it will be worth it in the end. Stay strong, believe in yourself, and choose to surround yourself with people who support and uplift you on your journey towards a better future.

As a side chick, don't stoop too low for anything just to get back to your glory. The attitude of using pregnancy, blackmailing, murder and others to get back to your former position shouldn't cross your mind. You need to know that in spite of the above behavior of yours, it's left for the man to decide on whether to accept you back or not. And don't ever forget that he is dealing with your past, wrestling with fear and confusion of where he is at now. His heart is locked, and he sees your attempt as a disruption to his life. The decision all lies on you as to whether you would be a home healer or a home wrecker. You need to make a decision for restoration and understand that true change comes from within. Reflect on your actions and strive for personal growth and maturity, rather than resorting to desperate measures.

Now, there are some spouses who are demanding, controlling, and abusive with their words towards their partners. They always love to put the other spouse in a box, criticizing every mistake of theirs and taking them for granted. These spouses don't realize what they are doing to themselves. They are simply making way for themselves, into becoming the mistress. This toxic behavior not only affects their current relationship but can have long-term consequences on their mental and emotional well-being. It is essential for these individuals to seek help and work on their communication skills to build a healthier relationship.

I was having a conversation with a guy that I met sometime ago, and our discussion seemed to be going in the right direction. In the process of the discussion, he told me that his marriage would break if he happens to bring his daughter that was born to him by another woman to live with him under the same roof with the current wife. This revelation made me realize how complex and fragile relationships can be, especially when past decisions and actions come into play. You see, this woman didn't realize what she was doing to herself. Instead of choosing to be ruled by love and compassion in her family, she decided to choose the opposite, which is the path that has led many people to become a side chick. This choice not only affects her happiness but also the stability and harmony of her household.

Never forget where you were coming from and where God picked you up from. Wherever you are now is a result of God's grace, not by your own power. God, at a certain time, had to remind King Saul, how humble he was before he became a king. He is also reminding you today where He picked you up from, and the need for you to be humble. Always remember to stay grounded and grateful for the blessings in your life, recognizing that they are gifts and not entitlements.

Many people were humble before they got married. Now, they have become proud, looking down on people that are either unmarried or divorced. They easily forget the old saying that, "Today is for me, but tomorrow is for you." Let us remain humble, irrespective of whatever we are and have. The book of Job 1:21 tells us that the Lord giveth and He taketh. Learn to live as if you have nothing, even though you may have everything. Everything you have can be taken away from you in seconds, and you would find yourself on the other side. This mindset will help you appreciate what you have and treat others with respect and kindness.

Also, there are second men who were the first men or used to be the first men in their women's lives that are playing the same role of being a mistress now. There are men who are ruled by their pride, just like we have the women that are ruled by their emotions and feelings. These men, too, need to evaluate their actions and understand the impact of their behavior on their relationships. By fostering humility and self-awareness, both men and women can work towards healthier and more fulfilling partnerships.

We should also remember that humility is not a sign of weakness, but rather a strength. It takes courage to admit when we are wrong and to ask for forgiveness. Humility allows us to grow and improve as individuals and strengthens our relationships with others. As Proverbs 16:18 says, "Pride goes before destruction, a haughty spirit before a fall." Let us strive to cultivate humility in all aspects of our lives.

In addition, being humble can also open doors for opportunities and blessings. When we are humble, we are more approachable, and others are more willing to work with us or help us. It also allows us to learn from others and expand our knowledge and skills. By being humble, we can create a positive impact on those around us and contribute to a more harmonious society.

Furthermore, humility is an important aspect of spiritual growth. It helps us recognize that we are not the center of the universe and that there is a higher power at work in our lives. It teaches us to trust in God's plan for us and to surrender our own desires and ambitions. As James 4:6 says, "God opposes the proud but shows favor to the humble." Let us strive to be humble in our faith and surrender to God's will.

In conclusion, humility is a crucial trait for both individuals and relationships. It allows us to become better versions of ourselves, fosters healthier connections with others, and helps us grow spiritually. Let us continue to cultivate humility in our lives and be open to the blessings it can bring. So let us practice humility in all aspects of our lives, knowing that it is a key ingredient for personal growth and fulfilling relationships.

No matter who we are or what roles we play in society, let us always remember the importance of humility and strive towards embodying this virtue every day.

Most of these men work so hard to provide everything that their families need. They go to great lengths to ensure that the physical and material necessities are met, often sacrificing their own time and energy to do so. However, most times, they just stop at that. The wives of these men are usually frustrated and emotionally down because their husbands fail to provide them with other needs that are not physical or that money can't buy, such as emotional support and companionship.

These men tend to overlook the fact that their wives need their encouragement, motivation, caring, and attention—needs of the heart that are just as important as any material provision. As they continue with this behavior, a time comes in the woman's life when she finally breaks down and decides to leave, making the man become a mistress to his own loneliness.

Now, the woman has moved on with her life, and so has the man, albeit in different directions. But later on, this man comes to the painful realization that he has made a great mistake in his life. He now understands that his new-found ladies can't give him the special touch and treatment that his previous wife gave him. All that they could offer was sex, romance, and kissing, which pale in comparison to the deep emotional connection he once had.

Because of this, his life has taken a drastic turn for the worse. He is now either fat as a result of eating junk food or has become skinny by not eating well. This physical decline is a mere reflection of his inner turmoil. Now, he begins to see how important his former wife was in his life. He wants to return to his first position, to the life he once knew, but this woman reminds him of his disappointment, uncaring behavior, and other past failings.

Currently, someone else has recognized the gifts and special qualities in this woman and has acknowledged them, making her happy in her new marriage. This man in question is now doing everything possible, sending her flowers, calling her, but it's too late to work things out because she has moved on with her life. Someone else is now fulfilling the role he failed to.

There are some women who are willing and ready to be the side chicks when their role changes, hoping to get you back. On the other hand, there are some women who will never do so because they are being satisfied by their current partners. So, the guys who made the mistake of allowing their wives to go must know how to find a way out of her life and seek a way to heal themselves. You don't have to disrupt her life again with your selfishness. Your healing starts when you set your pride aside and learn to humble yourself. Only then will you begin to see the pathway to your own healing. When this happens, you will come to know that there are other good women out there who are waiting for you as you change your ways. If not, you will continue to waste away in your pride.

In Luke 17:27, the Bible says, "They ate; they drank; they married wives, and they were given in marriage, until the day that Noah entered the ark. And the flood came and destroyed them all." It's very clear from the above verse that people would be going in and out of relationships, and you would be bound to make the mistake of walking out of something valuable. "But do you know what?" It's much better to work things out with your spouse in your relationship than to walk out of it. The depression and pains associated with walking out can't be compared to the pain of the two of you trying to work things out.

Relationships require effort, understanding, and mutual respect. While the path of reconciliation may be challenging, it holds far more promise and fulfillment than the loneliness that follows separation. Taking the time to nurture and cherish your partner can lead to a deeper and more meaningful connection, one that endures through the trials and tribulations of life. So, before making any drastic decisions, consider the long-term impact on both your life and the life of your partner. It may be worth the effort to save and strengthen what you have, rather than starting anew with someone else.

Moreover, it's important to recognize that pride is often the root cause of relationship issues. It can prevent us from truly listening and understanding our partner's perspective, leading to misunderstandings and conflicts. Learning to let go of our egos and apologize when necessary can go a long way in creating a healthy and harmonious relationship.

In addition, communication plays a crucial role in maintaining a strong bond with your partner. Expressing your feelings openly and honestly, without attacking or blaming each other, can help resolve conflicts and deepen your connection. It's also essential to actively listen to your partner, showing empathy and trying to understand their point of view. By communicating effectively, you can build trust and create a safe space for open and honest conversations.

Lastly, it's crucial to continuously work on yourself and your relationship. Like any living being, relationships require care, attention, and effort to thrive. This means prioritizing quality time with your partner, making an effort to understand their needs and desires, and actively working on addressing any issues that may arise. By investing in the health of your relationship, you can enjoy a fulfilling partnership that stands the test of time.

In conclusion, while no relationship is perfect and challenges are inevitable, it's important to remember that a strong and healthy bond with your partner can be achieved through commitment, communication, and continuous effort. By recognizing the importance of these factors and actively working on them, you can build a lasting relationship that brings joy, love, and fulfillment into your life. So don't give up on your relationship easily – instead, put in the work and watch it grow into something beautiful. Keep striving for growth and nurturing your relationship, knowing that the journey is just as important as reaching the destination. No matter how long you have been together or what challenges may arise, remember to always cherish and appreciate the love you share with each other. By doing so, you can create a strong foundation for a lasting and fulfilling relationship.

Keep learning, growing, and communicating together with your partner – and watch your love flourish.

So while relationships may not always be easy, they are certainly worth it in the end. Keep working on building a strong bond with your partner and enjoy the journey together. With commitment, effective communication, and continuous effort, you can have a fulfilling and lasting relationship that brings joy into your life.

CHAPTER THREE

THE DANGERS OF THE LAST DAYS

Aside our earthly marriages and relationships, we also have the spiritual ones. This spiritual relationship is our union with Christ. This relationship with our maker is the focal target of the enemy. He wants to cause many people to remain in a state of spiritual mistress.

The Bible made it clear that on the last days, many people will depart from the faith, even not believing in marriage. 1Timothy 4: 1, 3 say's: "Now, the spirit expressly says that in the latter times, some will depart from the faith, giving heed to deceiving spirits and doctrines of the demons.

Verse three says, "Forbidding to marry, and commanding to abstain from foods which God created to be received with Thanksgiving by those who believe and know the truth"

It's not a surprising news to say that we are already in that time described by the Bible. And without any slightest doubt, this is the calculated agenda of the devil to cause many people to abandon their relationship or union with their first and true love, Jesus. The COVID 19 Pandemic that triggered the exodus or mass departure of many people from the church, is one of the powerful tools of the enemy in achieving his purpose of making many people remain the spiritual mistress.

Now, Jesus is saying, "I am married to the backsliders; but now, Satan is in control of their lives through fear, deception, and manipulation".

Satan now squeezes himself back in their lives, severing their relationship with God. But in this case, however, Jesus refuses to or can never be the mistress, because Satan has nothing on Him. Remember what happened in the book of Matthew chapter 4. He wanted to make Jesus fall down and worship him by offering him food, fame and authority. His plan was to severe the relationship that existed between Jesus and His father. He wanted to divert the loyalty and obedience of Jesus to the Father towards himself. He however forgot to understand that he has nothing on his own. It was the same thing that he stole from Adam and Eve that he tried to give back to Jesus. He practically forgot that it was the same God that handed over all the possessions of Adam and Eve to them at the first place.

Jesus owns everything, but Satan absolutely has nothing. To live for Satan is to settle for less and nothingness. That's the reason I can't tell why people heed to his ways and counsel. Remember that he is the mistress. He was the praise leader in Heaven, who was beautifully, fearfully and wonderfully made, according to the nature of God. He continued to occupy his position in Heaven as the praise leader until he looked right and envied the worship that was ascribed unto God. He lead years with envy in his heart, until he got so foolish and plotted to overthrow God, the king of glory.

But God knew his heart, and had already planned for His great salvation to be offered to everyone who would believe in Him. And that is why Jesus came to offer us freedom from our bondage in sin, so that we can live a life of righteousness and holiness.

When He died on the cross, He took away all our sins and gave us His righteousness. We are no longer slaves to sin but free to live according to the will of God. Satan may try to tempt us and deceive us, but we have the power to resist him and overcome him through Jesus Christ.

So let's not be deceived by Satan's lies and schemes. Let's remember that we are children of God, heirs to His kingdom, and co-heirs with Christ. We have been given authority over demonic forces through the name of Jesus. And when we submit ourselves to God and resist the devil, he will flee from us (James 4:7). We must also remember that Satan is a defeated foe. He may try to come against us, but he already knows his ultimate fate - eternal damnation in hell. But as for those who believe in Jesus and follow Him, we have the promise of eternal life in heaven.

Therefore, let us stand firm in our faith and trust in God, knowing that He has already won the victory over Satan through Jesus' death and resurrection. And as we continue to praise and worship God, let us do so with a heart full of love and thanksgiving for all that He has done for us. For we are truly blessed to be called children of God, led by the perfect praise leader - Jesus Christ. So let's continue to lift our voices in praise and adoration, glorifying His name forevermore. Amen.

As believers, we must also remember that although Satan is defeated, he can still try to deceive us through false teachings and false prophets. That's why it is crucial for us to stay rooted in the word of God and discern what is truth from what is a lie.

We must also be vigilant and on guard, not allowing ourselves to fall into temptation or stray away from the path that God has set before us. As 1 Peter 5:8 reminds us, "Be alert and of sober mind. Your enemy the devil prowls around like a roaring lion looking for someone to devour." But with our faith firmly rooted in Christ, we can stand strong against any attack from Satan.

Let us also remember that we are called to be a light in this dark world. As Ephesians 5:8 says, "For you were once darkness, but now you are light in the Lord. Live as children of light." We have been given the power and authority through Jesus to overcome any spiritual battle and shine God's love and truth to those around us.

So let us not be discouraged or afraid when faced with trials or attacks from the enemy. Instead, let us remember that we are more than conquerors through Christ who loves us (Romans 8:37) and continue to put on the full armor of God every day.

(Ephesians 6:11). And let our lives be a continuous praise and testimony to the power and goodness of our God, for all eternity. Amen.

Let us also not forget that as children of God, we are called to love one another just as He loves us. In John 13:34-35, Jesus commands us to "love one another. As I have loved you, so you must love one another. By this everyone will know that you are my disciples, if you love one another."

Now, Jesus is saying, "I am married to the backsliders; but now, Satan is in control of their lives through fear, deception, and manipulation".

Satan now squeezes himself back in their lives, severing their relationship with God. But in this case, however, Jesus refuses to or can never be the mistress, because Satan has nothing on Him. Remember what happened in the book of Matthew chapter 4. He wanted to make Jesus fall down and worship him by offering him food, fame and authority. His plan was to severe the relationship that existed between Jesus and His father. He wanted to divert the loyalty and obedience of Jesus to the Father towards himself. He however forgot to understand that he has nothing on his own. It was the same thing that he stole from Adam and Eve that he tried to give back to Jesus. He practically forgot that it was the same God that handed over all the possessions of Adam and Eve to them at the first place.

Jesus owns everything, but Satan absolutely has nothing. To live for Satan is to settle for less and nothingness. That's the reason I can't tell why people heed to his ways and counsel. Remember that he is the mistress. He was the praise leader in Heaven, who was beautifully, fearfully and wonderfully made, according to the nature of God. He continued to occupy his position in Heaven as the praise leader until he looked right and envied the worship that was ascribed unto God. He lead years with envy in his heart, until he got so foolish and plotted to overthrow God, the king of glory.

Sadly for him, Satan was thrown out of Heaven himself because of his rebellious act. It was so foolish of Satan to think that God was on the same level as him; the all-knowing God who sees all things and whose wisdom surpasses human understanding. Satan failed to comprehend that God would never create anything that could destroy Him. Throughout history, man's creations, such as towering skyscrapers, complex cars, and advanced machines, have often led to unintended consequences and destruction. However, God is fundamentally different; His perfection and omnipotence mean He cannot be undermined or overthrown. It's impossible for God to be subjugated; rather, we are the ones who can stray and fall. He remains God, sovereign and supreme, all alone by Himself.

It greatly benefits backsliders, who were once in a spiritual marriage with God, to return to Him through Jesus Christ. As a spiritual mistress, it is crucial to reconsider your ways and make a conscious decision to return to Him today. Unlike the devil, who is forever condemned and will never have the opportunity or privilege to repent, you have the chance to change your path. The devil is eternally trapped in his sin and destined for destruction, but you, on the other hand, have the choice and the time to repent and reconcile with your first love while you are still alive. Don't squander such a wonderful and rare opportunity.

Jesus is earnestly knocking at the door of your heart today.

Revelation 3:20 says, "Behold, I stand at the door and knock. If anyone hears my voice and opens the door, I will come into him and dine with him, and he with me." This scripture emphasizes the intimate relationship Jesus desires to have with each of us, symbolized by sharing a meal together.

The best decision you can make is to bring joy to Jesus by freely opening the door of your heart to Him once again. When He enters your life, He will bestow upon you peace, joy, and love that surpass all understanding. Remember this: no human being, regardless of their status or possessions, has the power to grant you such profound qualities except Jesus. His love is unmatched and His grace is sufficient for all your needs. Embrace this divine opportunity to renew your relationship with Him and experience the transformative power of His presence in your life.

Moreover, as a spiritual mistress, it is important to constantly seek guidance and wisdom from God. Proverbs 3:5-6 says, "Trust in the Lord with all your heart and lean not on your own understanding; in all your ways submit to him, and he will make your paths straight." By surrendering our own understanding and desires to God, we allow Him to guide us towards the path of righteousness and fulfillment.

As we continue on this journey with Jesus, it is also crucial to stay vigilant against temptations and attacks from the devil. 1 Peter 5:8 reminds us, "Be alert and of sober mind. Your enemy the devil prowls around like a roaring lion looking for someone to devour." The devil will stop at nothing to try and lead us away from God, but by staying rooted in prayer and studying the Word, we can stand strong against his schemes.

Finally, remember to always put Jesus first in all aspects of your life. Colossians 3:23 says, "Whatever you do, work at it with all your heart, as working for the Lord, not for human masters." No matter what challenges or struggles we may face, let us strive to honor God in everything we do. Let our lives be a reflection of His love and grace, as we continue to grow in our relationship with Him every day.

In conclusion, being a spiritual mistress means surrendering ourselves completely to Jesus and allowing Him to guide and transform us. Let us embrace this calling with open hearts and minds, constantly seeking His wisdom and protection against the schemes of the enemy. May our lives be a testament to His love and grace, as we live out our purpose as spiritual mistresses in this world. So let us continue to walk in faith, trusting in Him every step of the way. Amen.

Not even your earthly spouse or parents can provide you with spiritual blessings that come as a result of closeness to God. They might give you other things that money can buy, like material comforts and emotional support, but spiritual blessings are unique and divine gifts that only come from a deeper relationship with the Almighty.

The problem we often face is our doubt as to whether He really cares for us, especially when we are going through difficulties and suffering in our lives. This doubt is not new; you and I aren't the first people to exhibit this kind of attitude. Even Jesus' disciples in the boat believed in Him until they were hit by the storm. Just like many people today, the Bible states that while they were in the boat, things began to get rough and they asked Him if He cared whether they perished or not. But at the end of the day, He came to their rescue, calming the storm and proving that His care and power are constant.

Always remember that Jesus would never leave nor forsake you, even in your most difficult times. It might seem as though He doesn't care, but the truth remains that He's always there for you, no matter how dark it seems to be in your life. Jesus is the only way, the truth, and the life out of every predicament of yours. He is the guiding light that will lead you through the darkest valleys and the fiercest storms.

In the book of Mark, we see different kinds of people who approached Jesus for various life's issues ranging from healing, deliverance, compassion, forgiveness of their sins, and other needs. Jesus didn't hesitate in granting them compassion and mercy. If He would readily do that for them, then "why do you now have to allow the mistress to ride you?" Satan is full of anger and rage over you because of the intimacy you enjoy with God. Don't allow him to keep you in your mistress state by taking your eyes away from Him. Remember, Satan's ultimate goal is to separate you from the love and grace of God, to make you feel unworthy and distant.

It's high time you went back to the one you made your vow to, who is Jesus. He is the one who promised you that He would never leave you nor forsake you. And surely, He would do as He has promised you. Human beings may give you promises; but in most cases, they would not be able to fulfill them because of one challenge or another, or due to the limitations of human nature.

However, Jesus never fails to deliver on His promises. He is seated at the right-hand side of the Father, making intercession for us. It's practically impossible for Him to leave us. He never ceases from praying for us, even when you don't see Him or feel His presence. His love is unending, and His intercession is constant, ensuring that we are always covered by His grace and mercy.

The devil wants us to stay in the position of the mistress when we are supposed to be in the lead. Unfortunately, many of us are in a tail position in our lives, where he wants us to be. This is because he has taken control over our minds and actions. We have become "mummified zombies" as he had programmed. But when our minds are released, and we start seeing and hoping, then we can be sober enough to change our positions from mistress to married people. This transformation requires a renewed mind and a steadfast focus on the promises of God.

The body of Christ needs to remain focused and stop being drunk with the world system and influences. We believers need to seek God's kingdom and His system of operation, not that of the polluted world. We must strive to align our lives with His divine will, seeking His guidance and adhering to His principles. The world may offer temporary pleasures and distractions, but true fulfillment and peace come from walking in God's path. Let us be vigilant and steadfast, always seeking the kingdom of God and His righteousness, and all other things will be added unto us. Our position as believers is not to be followers of the world, but leaders and ambassadors of God's kingdom.

In conclusion, Jesus never fails in His promises. As believers, we must keep our minds renewed and focused on Him, resisting the temptation and distractions that come from the enemy. Let us strive to walk in alignment with God's will, seeking His kingdom above all else. With a steadfast faith and unwavering trust in Him, we can overcome any challenges or trials that come our way. So let us stand firm in our position as children of God, knowing that nothing can separate us from His love and grace. May we always be reminded of our true identity and purpose in Christ, as we continue to walk in victory and fulfill the plans and purposes He has for our lives. So let us keep pressing on towards the goal, eagerly anticipating the day when we will see Jesus face to face and hear Him say, "Well done, my good and faithful servant." Keep running the race with perseverance, knowing that our position as children of God is secure and eternal. And may we never forget that with God by our side, all things are possible. So let us live each day with a renewed mind, focused on seeking His kingdom and fulfilling our purpose as His ambassadors in this world. As we do so, we will experience the true abundance and peace that can only come from walking in alignment with God's perfect will. So let us continue to spread His love and light wherever we go, shining brightly for all to see and bringing glory to His name.

And may His kingdom come, and His will be done on earth as it is in heaven. Amen.

Not even your earthly spouse or parents can do so. They might give you other things that money can buy, such as gifts, comfort, and even financial stability, but not spiritual blessings that come as a result of closeness to God. These material comforts, while valuable, cannot fill the void that can only be satisfied by a deep, personal relationship with the divine. The problem we often face is that we doubt whether He truly cares for us, especially when we are going through difficulties and suffering in our lives. This doubt can cloud our judgment and weaken our faith, making us feel isolated and abandoned. But you and I aren't the first people to exhibit this kind of attitude. Even Jesus' disciples in the boat believed in Him until they were hit by the storm.

Just like many people today, the Bible says that while they were in the boat, the conditions began to worsen, and they asked Him if He cared whether they perished or not. The storm rocked their faith, filling them with fear and uncertainty. But at the end of the day, Jesus came to their rescue, calming the storm and restoring peace. This miraculous event serves as a powerful reminder that He is always in control, even when circumstances seem dire. Always remember that Jesus would never leave nor forsake you, even in your most difficult times. It might seem as though He doesn't care, but the truth remains that He is always there for you, no matter how dark it seems to be in your life.

Jesus is the only way, the truth, and the life out of every predicament you face. In the book of Mark, we witness different kinds of people approaching Jesus for various life issues ranging from healing, to deliverance, to compassion, to forgiveness of their sins, and much more. These accounts illustrate His boundless compassion and limitless power to transform lives. Jesus didn't hesitate in granting them compassion and mercy. If He would readily do that for them, "why do you now have to allow the mistress to ride you?" Satan is full of anger and rage over you because of the intimacy you enjoy with God. His primary tactic is to sow seeds of doubt and despair in your heart. Don't allow him to keep you in your mistress state by taking your eyes away from Jesus.

It's high time you went back to the one you made your vow to, who is Jesus. He is the one who promised you that He would never leave you nor forsake you. And surely, He would do as He has promised. Human beings may give you promises; but in most cases, they would not be able to fulfill them because of one challenge or the other. Life's uncertainties often hinder human commitments, but Jesus transcends these limitations. However, Jesus never fails to deliver on His promises. He is seated at the right-hand side of the Father, making intercession for us. His intercessory work is a testament to His enduring love and commitment. It's practically impossible for Him to leave us. He never ceases from praying for us, even when you don't see Him. This constant divine support should be a source of immense comfort and encouragement, reinforcing that we are never alone in our struggles. We have a faithful intercessor who knows our every need and is constantly working on our behalf.

In light of this, we are called to remain steadfast in our faith, trusting that Jesus is always with us and will never leave us. Our circumstances may change, people may disappoint us, but Jesus remains the same- yesterday, today, and forever. He is the anchor for our souls in the midst of life's storms. And as we continue to fix our eyes on Him, we will experience His boundless love and compassion in all aspects of our lives.

The devil wants us to stay in the position of the mistress when we are supposed to be the leaders in our own lives. Unfortunately, many of us are in a state of subservience, exactly where he wants us to be. This is because he has taken control over our minds and actions, manipulating us into believing we are less than we truly are. We have become "mummified zombies" as he has programmed us to be, moving through life without truly living. But when our minds are released, and we start seeing and hoping, then we can be sober enough to change our positions from mistress to married people, taking on the role of leaders and fully embracing our faith.

The body of Christ needs to remain focused and stop being intoxicated with the world's systems and influences, which are often deceptive and misleading. We who are believers need to seek God's kingdom and His system of operation, not that of the polluted world. We must continually strive to align ourselves with His teachings, allowing our thoughts and actions to be guided by His divine wisdom and love. It's a journey of faith, trust, and unwavering commitment to the one who never fails us. As we walk this journey with Jesus, our minds will be renewed and transformed, and we will begin to see ourselves as God sees us—capable, beloved, and empowered.

We are not just mere servants or followers; we are sons and daughters of the Most High. We have been given authority through Christ to overcome the devil's schemes and stand firm in our faith. It is time for us to fully embrace our identity in Christ and walk in the power He has given us. Let us no longer live in fear or doubt, but instead, boldly declare our victory in Him. With this mentality, you would find it difficult to succumb to the giant in front of you, for you are the giant in your mind.

Consider how a massive one-ton elephant can be controlled by a mere hundred-pound man. This control is established when the elephant is young. A chain is placed around the baby elephant's foot, and even when the chain is later removed, the elephant remains mentally bound, believing it is still trapped. Similarly, the devil ties our minds for so long that we are controlled by invisible satanic forces, even when Jesus has set us free. Beloved, take up Jesus' word and act on it. You are already free in Him. Keep confessing and affirming it, both secretly and openly. Christ has given you all things that pertain to life and godliness. Walk in the freedom that has been bestowed upon you.

I know a guy who rented one of my apartments, and who is highly irritated with God for seemingly no reason. He claimed that he had been dead thirteen times and that it was the devil who brought him back to life each time. Recently, he had another near-death experience and claimed it was the devil who saved him a fourteenth time. I asked him why he hates God and loves Satan, giving the praises due to God to the devil instead. He couldn't provide a coherent answer, which further highlighted the confusion and manipulation in his mind.

We must remember that Christ has given us all things that pertain to life and godliness. By embracing this truth and walking in the freedom He offers, we can live our lives with purpose and power, unfettered by the chains that previously held us back. The devil may try to deceive us and keep us bound in bondage, but we have the authority given to us by Jesus to resist and reject his lies. We can confidently walk in our true identity as children of God, knowing that we are free from any mental or spiritual restraints.

So let us continue to renew our minds daily with the word of God and stand firm against the schemes of the enemy. Let us not be like the elephant, still mentally bound when we have already been set free by Jesus. Instead, let us boldly proclaim our freedom and live according to our true nature as heirs of God's kingdom.

Satan is the least, while God is the greater. Choose God today and your life would turn out to be the best.

Marriage is a sacred institution. It's represented by the Trinity-the union that God has with God the Son and God the Holy Spirit from creation. It's God's intention that we can look at the bond or union that exists among these three but same personality and be like them.

But Satan's intention is to make mockery of marriages. We must be spiritual to understand how the devil operates against marriage. He doesn't mind if you are together with your spouse financially. As far as two of you are not together in one mind or emotionally, he would succeed in penetrating into your union. He hates relationship with great vengeance. That's why he tries to give some of us that are married and pleasing God, the reason we should leave our spouse.

He's a great liar. The Bible describes him as the Father of all lies in John 8:44. He has talked many people out of their relationships. To survive in our marriages and relationships, we have to be more spiritual than ever. 1Timothy 4:1 says, "Now the spirit speaketh expressly that in the latter times some shall depart from the faith, giving heed to seducing spirits and doctrines of the devil." Page | 26

As believers, we must be aware of the spiritual warfare that is constantly happening in our marriages and relationships. The enemy will use any means necessary to bring division and discord between partners, whether it's through financial struggles, misunderstandings, or even outside temptations.

But as children of God, we have the power to overcome these attacks. We can pray for protection over our marriages and ask God to give us wisdom in handling conflicts. We can also seek guidance from wise and godly mentors who can provide support and counsel during difficult times.

CHAPTER - FOUR

DEMONIC OPPRESSION IN MARRIAGE

It's important to remember that marriage is a reflection of God's love for us. Just as He is faithful and committed to us, we should strive to be faithful and committed to our spouses. This means being intentional about nurturing our relationship, communicating effectively, and prioritizing our partner's needs above our own.

As we continue on this journey of marriage, let us always seek God's guidance and trust in His plan for our union. Let us also remember that the enemy may try to sow seeds of doubt or discord, but with God on our side, we have nothing to fear.

So let us stand firm in faith, knowing that no weapon formed against our marriages will prosper. And when challenges arise, let us cling to the promises of God and hold fast to our commitment to each other.

May our marriages be a testament of God's love and grace, and may we continue to grow together in His perfect plan for our lives. As it says in Ecclesiastes 4:12, "Though one may be overpowered, two can defend themselves. A cord of three strands is not quickly broken." Let us keep God at the center of our marriage, knowing that with Him, we are stronger together.

This concludes our discussion on marriage from a spiritual perspective but there is always more to learn and discover as we continue to grow in our relationships with God and each other. So let us continue to seek wisdom, communicate openly and love unconditionally as we journey through the beautiful gift of marriage. Let us also remember to pray for all marriages around the world, that they may be filled with God's love, grace, and strength. May our unions be a reflection of God's perfect plan for love and partnership.

As Christians, we are called to be a light in this world and that includes our marriages. By choosing to honor God in our relationship, we can inspire others and show them the beauty of a Christ-centered marriage.

Now, there are demons who use a piece of truth about your spouse to consume you with lies. They whisper insidious falsehoods into your mind, playing on your insecurities and doubts. If you are not spiritually mature enough, then you will take the bait, and this will lead to the crashing of your relationship. The manipulation is subtle at first, but it grows stronger, feeding on your pride and unchecked emotions. Afterward, these demons would leave you lonely and depressed, wondering what you have done to yourself and your once-happy relationship.

This is because you were taken over by a demon who used your pride and emotion to get into your life and cause you to make bad decisions. These decisions, influenced by negative forces, push you further away from the virtues needed to sustain a healthy relationship.

Now, all you are left with is depression and regrets, instead of long-suffering and patience with your partner. As a result, you now become moved by revenge and anger, causing you to leave your marriage. This impulsive act of leaving is not a solution but a reaction to the manipulation you've undergone. And currently, you are being bound by the spirit of mistress, a spirit that thrives on broken commitments and unfulfilled promises.

I know it takes two people to stay happily and successfully married. Both partners must be committed to working through their issues and understanding each other deeply. I am equally aware that you can't force anyone to stay with you in any relationship, nor should you ever endure an abusive relationship. It is important to recognize the difference between normal marital strife and harmful situations that necessitate separation. I know of all these situations that might want to make us relinquish our relationships. External pressures, personal failings, and misunderstandings do threaten our lawful marriages and relationships. But all I am saying is that we should try to stay together and seek to resolve our issues before we jump to leave each other.

Stop using the guest room when the two of you are having problems. This physical separation only amplifies emotional distance. Always remember that the guest room is made for visitors, not for you who are lawfully married, unless there is consent from your spouse to do so for a moment. Communication and togetherness are key, even in times of conflict. Instead, use these difficult moments as opportunities to grow closer and understand each other's perspectives. By addressing issues head-on and staying united, you strengthen the bond that holds your marriage together.

Another essential aspect of maintaining a healthy marriage is taking care of yourself. It's easy to prioritize work, kids, and other responsibilities over self-care, but neglecting your own well-being can lead to resentment and burnout. Make time for yourself to do the things you love and that make you feel good. This could be exercising, pursuing a hobby, or simply taking a relaxing bath. When you take care of your own needs, you are better able to show up as your best self in your relationship.

It's also crucial to keep the romance alive in your marriage. As time goes by and life gets busier, it's natural for the initial spark to fade. But that doesn't mean you can't reignite it. Plan date nights, surprise each other with small gestures of love and affection, and make an effort to keep the passion alive in your relationship. Showing appreciation and making your partner feel loved is crucial for a lasting marriage.

In addition to these practical steps, seeking help from a therapist or counselor can also be beneficial. A neutral third party can help facilitate communication and provide tools for resolving conflicts effectively. Don't view going to therapy as a sign of weakness; instead, see it as a proactive step towards improving your relationship.

Lastly, remember to always be open and honest with your partner. Communication is key in any marriage, and being able to express your feelings and concerns openly can help prevent issues from escalating. Don't shy away from difficult conversations, but approach them with empathy and a willingness to listen and understand each other's perspectives.

In conclusion, marriage takes effort, dedication, and constant communication. By prioritizing the health of your relationship, taking care of yourself, keeping the romance alive, seeking outside help when needed, and maintaining open communication with your partner, you can build a strong foundation for a lasting and fulfilling marriage. Remember that it's okay to make mistakes, as long as you learn from them and use them to grow together as a couple. So don't give up when faced with challenges; instead, face them head-on with love, understanding, and a commitment to keeping your marriage strong. With these principles in mind, you can create a happy and fulfilling marriage that will last for years to come.

Keep learning and growing together, never stop working on your relationship, and always cherish the love you have for each other. Marriage is a journey full of ups and downs, but by staying committed to each other and the bond you share, you can weather any storm and come out stronger on the other side. So, embrace the challenges, celebrate the joys, and keep building a marriage that is built to last. Remember, love is not just a feeling; it's an action that requires constant effort and nurturing. Let your marriage be a reflection of your love for each other and never stop investing in its growth and strength. With these tips in mind, you can create a successful and fulfilling marriage that will stand the test of time. Here's to many years of happiness with your partner by your side! Cheers to a thriving marriage filled with love, trust, communication, and endless growth. May your marriage be a source of joy, support, and comfort for both of you as you navigate through life together. Always remember that a strong and healthy marriage is not just about the big moments or grand gestures; it's about the small everyday actions and choices that show your love, commitment, and dedication to each other. So keep loving, keep growing, and keep building a marriage that is truly built to last. With these tips in mind, you can create a successful and fulfilling marriage that will stand the test of time.

Be quick to forgive your spouse as much as it lies within you, and as much as the Lord would help you. Learn to look at your spouse through the eyes of Jesus, especially when they make a mistake that you are finding it difficult to forgive or let go. Just think of how many times you have offended God and asked Him for forgiveness. And He readily granted you the forgiveness you sought. Do the same to your spouse. Forgiveness is a cornerstone of any healthy relationship and is vital for maintaining harmony and understanding.

Regrettably, I have seen people who walked away from their relationships and then fell into depression. They thought that it was going to be quite easier to walk away. What they didn't realize is that the pain of separation can be more devastating than the conflicts they faced. If you know that you are not going to be the mistress, then, you must make a solid choice today. Even in the midst of your stubbornness and fluctuating emotions, ensure you make the right decision to work out your relationship so that you won't become the mistress. Staying committed and working through challenges can lead to a deeper and more fulfilling connection.

Don't rely on the sayings or some defenses that some people put up just to find an exit route from their relationships. Don't say that you were convinced that your marriage was lust, and not love at first sight; or that there was no connection between the two of you; or even that no iota of love existed, just a sexual relationship between you and your spouse. Never buy into these ideologies as a means of stepping out of your relationship. You would be doing yourself much more harm than good by reaching and taking this type of decision. Some marriages can be salvaged through patience, counseling, and mutual effort.

Remember, relationships require continuous effort and understanding. There will be ups and downs, but with a commitment to growth and the willingness to forgive, you can build a lasting and loving partnership. Be proactive in seeking solutions and always communicate openly with your spouse. The journey may not always be easy, but it will be worth it in the end. Don't let the pain of separation be your story, instead, let the strength of your commitment and love be the foundation of a lasting and fulfilling relationship.

It is important to remember that relationships are not perfect and require continuous effort to maintain. It is common for couples to face challenges and conflicts, but it is how they handle these difficulties that truly defines the strength of their relationship. Communication, understanding, and forgiveness are essential components in building a successful partnership.

In addition to working through challenges together, it is also crucial for individuals to make conscious decisions about their relationship. This includes being honest with oneself about one's feelings and needs, as well as being open and transparent with one's partner. It is important to continuously evaluate the health of the relationship and make adjustments as needed.

Moreover, it is important for individuals to prioritize their own personal growth and happiness within a relationship. This means maintaining separate identities and pursuing individual interests, while also supporting each other in achieving personal goals. A healthy balance of independence and togetherness can strengthen a relationship and prevent feelings of resentment or suffocation.

In summary, relationships require effort, understanding, forgiveness, honesty, and continuous evaluation in order to thrive. Marriage does not guarantee a perfect path without challenges, but with mutual commitment and a strong foundation, individuals can create a fulfilling and lasting partnership. So don't let the end of a relationship mark the end of your story, instead use it as an opportunity to grow and build something even stronger. Keep writing your love story, one chapter at a time. So keep working on yourself and your relationship, because in the end, it's not about reaching the finish line but enjoying the journey together. Don't let 'the end' be an ending, but rather a new beginning for both individuals to continue growing and loving each other. Always remember that true love never ends, it simply evolves and grows stronger over time. Embrace the challenges, celebrate the joys, and cherish every moment spent with your partner.

Additionally, it is important to remember that each relationship is unique and there is no one-size-fits-all formula for success. Communication, compromise, and commitment are key components of a healthy and thriving relationship, but what works for one couple may not work for another. It is important to find what works best for you and your partner, while also being open to trying new things and adapting as needed.

Furthermore, navigating through conflicts and disagreements in a relationship can be challenging. However, it is important to remember that these challenges can also be opportunities for growth and understanding. Instead of avoiding or suppressing conflict, approach it with a willingness to listen and understand each other's perspectives. This allows for open and honest communication, leading to resolution and ultimately strengthening the relationship.

In conclusion, relationships are continuously evolving journeys that require effort, dedication, and adaptability. By embracing the ups and downs, communicating effectively, and constantly working on oneself and the relationship, individuals can create a strong and lasting partnership filled with love, growth, and happiness. So keep writing your love story, one chapter at a time. The end is just the beginning of a new and exciting adventure with your partner. So keep writing, and may your love story be filled with endless chapters of love, joy, and growth. So remember to always cherish the moments, face the challenges together, and never stop growing in love - because true love is forever.

Some marriages were simply put together by Satan to mock God's intention concerning relationships, bringing confusion into them and discouraging many people from getting married. I myself never thought I would be married. The race to the altar and then to the court for divorce was very discouraging to me until I found the glue that holds marriages together from tearing apart. The glue is no other person than Jesus Christ. When Christ is the glue that holds your marriage, there is a willingness to be together and make your marriage work.

Always keep in mind that when you get married, the devil will continue to fight your desire to be with each other. That's the major reason Apostle Paul advises believers to always be together. In 1 Corinthians 7:5, he says, "Don't deprive one another except with consent for a time, that you may give yourselves to fasting and prayer, and come together again, so that Satan doesn't tempt you because of your lack of self-control."

Satan's intention is to pull you apart from each other. Just imagine some of the couples who are divorced now. There was a time when they couldn't keep their hands off each other. There was a time in their lives when they couldn't wait to walk down the aisle. Some of them even brought forward their wedding dates just to get hooked together quickly. These couples had wonderful plans on how to make their relationships work out. However, their expectations easily crumbled when they hit a speed bump.

Marital challenges often stem from communication breakdowns, financial stress, or differing life goals. For instance, a couple might struggle to manage their finances, leading to constant arguments and tension. Another might disagree on whether to have children, which can cause significant emotional strain. These issues, compounded with daily stressors, can create a fertile ground for Satan's interference.

When couples fail to address these problems early on, they might start feeling disconnected and resentful. In such moments, it's easy for negative influences to take root. That's why it's crucial for couples to stay connected through open communication, mutual respect, and shared spiritual practices. Regularly praying together and seeking guidance from God can help reinforce the bond and provide clarity during tough times.

Moreover, seeking counsel from trusted spiritual advisors or participating in marriage enrichment programs can offer additional support. Such resources provide tools and strategies to navigate marital challenges effectively. By staying proactive and nurturing their relationship, couples can safeguard their marriage against Satan's attempts to create division.

In conclusion, while Satan aims to disrupt and destroy marriages, turning to Christ and building a strong spiritual foundation can help couples withstand these attacks. By continually working on their relationship and seeking divine guidance, they can maintain a loving and lasting union. Let us remember that God designed marriage to be a sacred and beautiful union, and with His help, we can overcome any obstacle that comes our way. So let's keep the faith and trust in Him to protect and strengthen our marriages. Throughout this content, we have discussed the various ways in which Satan can attack marriages and how couples can protect their relationship from these attacks. However, it's essential to note that every couple's situation is unique, and there is no one-size-fits-all solution.

For some couples, seeking individual counseling or therapy might be necessary to address deeper underlying issues. For others, reading books on healthy communication and conflict resolution may be beneficial. The key is to be open to seeking help and continuously working on improving the relationship.

Additionally, it's important for couples to remember that marriage is a journey, and there will be bumps along the way. It's essential to approach these challenges with patience, understanding, and grace towards one another. Remembering that your spouse is not your enemy but your partner in navigating life together can help strengthen the bond between you.

Lastly, never underestimate the power of forgiveness in a marriage. As humans, we are bound to make mistakes, but choosing to forgive and move forward can bring healing and growth to a relationship. It's not easy, but with God's help, forgiveness can mend even the most broken of marriages.

In conclusion, while Satan may try to attack and destroy marriages, there is hope for couples who are willing to put in the effort and trust in God. With His guidance and grace, marriages can withstand any attack and continue to thrive. Let us always remember that marriage is a sacred bond designed by God, and with Him at the center, it can truly be a beautiful reflection of His love. So let's commit to continually working on our marriages, seeking help when needed, showing grace and forgiveness, and trusting in God's plan for our relationships. No matter the challenges we may face, with God's help, our marriages can become sources of joy, growth, and deep love that lasts a lifetime. Let us hold onto hope and keep fighting for strong and healthy marriages.

We must also remember to support and encourage other couples in their marriages. We are not meant to go through this journey alone, and by building a community of married couples who uplift and pray for one another, we can strengthen the institution of marriage as a whole.

Lastly, may we always strive to put God at the center of our marriages, for He is the foundation of true and lasting love. Whether we are newlyweds or celebrating decades of marriage, let us never stop seeking His guidance and allowing Him to work in our relationships. With God at the helm, our marriages can truly be a beautiful testament to His faithfulness and love. So let us hold onto hope, trust in His plan, and continue to build strong and thriving marriages that bring glory to God.

Additional tips for a successful marriage

- In addition to the important aspects mentioned above, here are some extra tips for building a strong and successful marriage:
- Communication: It is essential to have open and honest communication in marriage. This means actively listening, expressing your thoughts and feelings, and working through conflicts together.
- Quality time: Make sure to prioritize spending quality time with your partner. This can include date nights, regular check-ins, or simply setting aside uninterrupted time for each other.
- Respect: Show respect for your partner's thoughts, opinions, and boundaries. This creates a safe and trusting environment within the marriage.
- Gratitude: Expressing gratitude towards your partner for the little things they do can go a long way in showing appreciation and strengthening your bond.
- Compromise: Marriage requires compromise and being willing to meet halfway on certain issues. Remember that you are a team, and your partner's happiness and well-being should also be important to you.
- Forgiveness: No marriage is perfect, and conflicts will arise. It is important to practice forgiveness and work through issues instead of holding grudges.

- Self-care: Taking care of yourself physically, mentally, and emotionally can benefit both you and your marriage. When you feel your best, it can positively impact your relationship with your partner.
- Embrace change: As individuals, we are constantly growing and evolving. Embracing change in ourselves and our partners can lead to a stronger and more fulfilling marriage.
- Have fun: Don't forget to have fun and enjoy each other's company! Laughter and shared experiences can help keep the spark alive in your relationship.

Remember, building a successful marriage takes effort from both partners. Continuously working on these aspects can help create a strong foundation for your relationship and lead to a happy and fulfilling partnership. So, always strive to make your marriage a top priority and never stop investing in it.

Now, all those plans of theirs—holding hands together in the park, seeing their dreams come to pass, and others—have gone sour and bitter. They have suddenly become worst enemies. And I find it pretty difficult to understand the idea of many people who claim to be good friends now that they are divorced, but who were like cats and rats when they were in a lawful union. It's a curious phenomenon. In fact, that's another name for mistress, who's the side chick.

I met a guy who had to put off a life-saving surgery just because he was not married. The performance of the surgery requires someone to take care of him during the recovery period. This guy in question just decided to marry for the purpose of finding someone that would take care of him. You see, this man was driven into the marriage as a result of selfishness. He didn't care about love or companionship; he just needed a caretaker. This singular reason is why many end up having mistresses today.

I know of another man, whose name I am not going to mention for some reason, that decided he was getting old, and based on that reason, he needed someone to push him around in a wheelchair. He got married because of this selfish attitude, not that he really wanted to do so. His marriage, too, was driven by necessity rather than genuine affection.

I was informed by a nurse, also, that there are many men in the hospital who are lonely and suffering from different illnesses. And there's no one to comfort them, just because of their singleness. Most of them decided not to enter into any relationship for reasons best known to them. But then, we need to know that being single is a cost, just like being in a relationship carries its own costs. Some men prefer their independence, but this choice can lead to isolation, especially in times of sickness or old age.

The complexities of human relationships often lead to unexpected and sometimes unfortunate outcomes, but understanding the motivations behind these choices can provide us with a deeper insight into the human condition. It is important to recognize that while some people may enter into relationships for selfish reasons, others do so out of a genuine desire for companionship and love. And in both cases, there are potential risks and rewards.

Furthermore, being single can also have its benefits. Many individuals find fulfillment and happiness in living an independent life, free from the responsibilities and challenges of a romantic relationship. They have more time and energy to pursue their passions, goals, and personal growth.

But regardless of one's relationship status, it is crucial to have a strong support system during times of need. This is where friends, family members or even hired caregivers play a vital role. It is important to have people who can provide emotional support, assist with daily tasks and offer companionship when needed.

In the end, whether one chooses to be single or enter into a relationship, the most important thing is finding fulfillment and happiness in life. Both options come with their own set of challenges and rewards, but what truly matters is making choices that align with one's values and desires. As humans, our need for companionship may vary, but what remains constant is our need for love and understanding from those around us. So let us strive to have meaningful connections and relationships in our lives, whether romantic or platonic, and make the most out of them. Let us also remember to never judge others for their choices in relationships, as we all have different experiences and motivations that shape our decisions. Instead, let us show empathy and support towards one another on this journey called life. So let's continue to celebrate the diversity of relationships and the beauty of human connections.

We live in a world where societal pressure often dictates what is considered "normal" when it comes to relationships. However, it is important to recognize that there is no one-size-fits-all formula for happiness in love. What works for one person may not work for another, and that is perfectly okay. It is important to break free from societal expectations and norms and instead focus on what truly makes us happy.

Another aspect of relationships that often goes overlooked is the importance of self-love. Before we can have a healthy relationship with someone else, we must first have a healthy relationship with ourselves. This means understanding our own needs, setting boundaries, and practicing self-care. Only when we are in a good place mentally, emotionally, and physically can we fully give ourselves to another person.

In conclusion, whether single or in a relationship, it is important to prioritize love and connection in our lives. Let us continue to challenge societal norms, embrace diversity, and practice self-love as we navigate the complex world of relationships. And above all, let us never forget the power of human connection and its ability to bring joy, fulfillment, and meaning to our lives. So here's to celebrating love in all its forms and spreading it wherever we go. Keep loving, keep connecting, keep thriving.

Each one has its own pain. Marriage, nevertheless, is not and should not be for selfish people. In every relationship, vows are usually made by each spouse to the other person. These vows are promises of commitment, love, support, and fidelity, intended to bind the couple together through the good times and the bad. Each person, however, is responsible for fulfilling their own vows in such a relationship. It's the lack of the fulfillment of these vows that leads to separation and bitterness, as unmet promises create dissatisfaction and disillusionment.

You need to know that it's the vow that keeps or holds the relationship together, not love alone. Love has to do with emotions, and emotions are inherently fluctuating. One day you might feel intensely in love, and the next day, due to stress or conflict, those feelings might wane. Commitment, on the other hand, has to do with responsibility and consistent effort. It's about choosing to stay and work things out, even when feelings are fleeting. Also, while love grows and evolves over time, commitment is about the present action—choosing every day to honor the bond you share.

Every relationship that lasted for a long time has to do with a great level of commitment, and not just love alone. The reason being that love, as wonderful and magical as it can be, easily vanishes away in the face of challenges and routine. It's commitment that makes spouses stay together, even when there are mistakes, misunderstandings, or periods of stagnation. Commitment is the glue that holds the relationship together, pushing through the tough times and rejoicing in the good ones.

As we grow in the Lord, it becomes much easier to remain together. Spiritual growth fosters qualities like patience, forgiveness, and unconditional love, which are crucial for a lasting relationship. You don't have to be worried about growing together in your marriage when both of you are growing together in Jesus. When a couple is united in their faith, they share a common goal and a set of values that guide their actions and decisions. It becomes easier and effortless to face life's challenges together, with a shared belief that God is at the center of their union.

Growing in Jesus is what keeps relationships stronger and healthier. His teachings and example provide a blueprint for a loving, selfless partnership. Remember that Jesus' name is a strong tower. You and your spouse would be preserved and protected from the calamities that hit relationships when you seek refuge in His name and under His divine covering. In times of crisis or doubt, turning to faith can provide hope, resilience, and a deeper connection. Ultimately, a marriage built on the foundation of faith, commitment, and mutual effort is one that can withstand the test of time. So, continue to grow in the Lord and make Him the center of your relationship.

Don't forget to also prioritize communication and intentional effort in your marriage. It's important to regularly check-in with each other, discuss any issues or concerns, and actively work on strengthening your relationship. Open and honest communication helps build trust, understanding, and a deeper emotional connection.

Additionally, showing appreciation and affection towards each other is crucial in maintaining a healthy and happy marriage. Small acts of kindness, words of affirmation, and physical touch can go a long way in making your partner feel loved and valued.

Remember that every relationship will face challenges, but how you face them and work through them together is what truly matters. Keep your faith in God and each other, and continue to grow and learn as individuals and as a couple. With perseverance, love, and faith, your marriage can continue to thrive for years to come.

So let us always strive towards building strong marriages rooted in the teachings of Jesus, filled with love, communication, and mutual effort. And may we always remember that with God at the center of our relationships, anything is possible. Let us continue to support one another on this journey of growing in Christ together as husband and wife. As the Bible says in Ecclesiastes 4:9-10, "Two are better than one, because they have a good return for their labor: If either of them falls down, one can help the other up. But pity anyone who falls and has no one to help them up." So let us be each other's support system, helping each other grow in our faith and marriage every day.

In conclusion, marriage is a beautiful journey that requires constant effort, communication, and faith. As Christians, we have the added blessing of having God as our foundation and guide. With His love and grace, we can overcome any challenges and continue to strengthen our marriages. Let us always strive towards building strong, loving, and God-centered marriages that can weather any storm. So let us continue to grow in love, faith, and unity as we journey through this wonderful gift of marriage together. Remember to always put God and your spouse first, and may His blessings be upon your marriage now and forevermore.

As Christians, it is important for us to also seek guidance from the Bible on how to maintain a healthy marriage. Some key teachings include selflessness, forgiveness, and communication. As we continue to live out these principles in our marriages, we can build a strong foundation that will withstand any trials that come our way.

Let us also not forget the importance of seeking help and advice from other Christian couples who have been married for many years. They can offer valuable wisdom and insights on how to navigate through different challenges and maintain a loving and God-honoring marriage.

As we continue to journey through life with our spouses, let us always remember to pray for one another and for our marriage. Prayer is a powerful tool that can strengthen our bond and help us overcome any obstacles. Let us also be each other's support system, always being there to lift each other up during difficult times and celebrate together during the good times.

Marriage is a beautiful gift from God that requires constant nourishment and care. Let us cherish this gift and continue to grow in our faith and marriage every day. May God bless all marriages with love, joy, and unwavering commitment. So let us walk hand in hand with our spouses, trusting in God's plan for our lives as we journey towards eternity together. So let us daily strive towards building strong foundations of love, trust, and faith in our marriages, always seeking guidance from the Word of God and the support of our Christian community. Together, with God at the center of our relationships, we can overcome any challenges and experience a truly fulfilling marriage that reflects His love for us. So let us continue to prioritize our relationship with God and our spouses above all else, trusting in His perfect timing and plan for our lives. Let us be reminded that with God's blessings upon our marriages, we can overcome any obstacle and thrive in a strong and loving union until eternity.

In conclusion, as Christians, let us always strive to put God at the center of our marriages, walking in love and faithfulness towards one another. Let us continuously seek His guidance and strength to build a lasting and fulfilling marriage that brings glory to His name. And may we never forget the power of prayer in nurturing and strengthening our relationships. May God bless all marriages and guide us in living out His perfect plan for our lives together as husband and wife. So let us always remember that with God's grace, love, and guidance, we can have a happy and fulfilling marriage that reflects His everlasting love for us. So let us continue to hold on to our faith and trust in God, knowing that He is with us every step of the way. And may our marriages always be a testament to His goodness and faithfulness. Let us never forget the importance of seeking God's will and walking in obedience to Him as we journey through life together with our spouses. May our marriages be a reflection of His love and grace, and a source of joy, strength, and support for each other. So let us keep on building strong foundations, nurturing our relationships with love and trust, all for the glory of God.

As we navigate the ups and downs of marriage, let us also remember to extend grace and forgiveness to our spouses, just as God has shown us grace and forgiveness. Let us not hold onto grudges or let pride get in the way of a healthy and thriving marriage. Instead, let us humbly seek reconciliation and work through any conflicts with love and understanding.

And in times of struggle or difficulty, may we lean on each other for support and comfort, but most importantly, may we turn to God in prayer together. For when we pray as a couple, we invite God into our marriage and allow Him to guide us towards unity and strength.

In the end, may our marriages be a reflection of the ultimate love story between Christ and His church, constantly pointing others towards the beauty and power of God's love. So let us never stop growing in our faith and in our love for each other as we continue to walk hand in hand with God by our side. Trusting in His perfect plan for our marriages and finding joy in every season of life together. Let us always give thanks to Him for the gift of marriage and strive to honor Him through it all.

As we conclude this guide, remember that marriage is a lifelong journey filled with blessings, challenges, and growth. But with God at the center, anything is possible. So let us continue to seek His wisdom and guidance, constantly striving to become the best spouses we can be for each other.

May this guide serve as a reminder and encouragement for all married couples, and may it bring glory to God who has brought us together in love. Let us cherish our marriages and always strive towards building stronger foundations, trusting in God's faithfulness every step of the way. So here's to a lifetime of love, commitment, and growth in marriage – all for the glory of God. Amen.

32.In Ecclesiastes 4:12, the Bible says, "Though one may be overpowered, two can defend themselves. A cord of three strands is not easily broken." This profound statement takes us back to the relationship the Trinity have in Genesis, when they say, "Let us make man in our own image and likeness." Here, we witness an eternal relationship that continuously grows in perfect unity and bond, showcasing the divine harmony and cooperation within the Godhead.

This image of unity is a model for how God wants us to be in our relationships. That's why, when we take vows, we make solemn declarations such as "until death do us part." These vows are not to be taken lightly; they signify a lifelong commitment that should not be easily abandoned when the inevitable challenges of marriage arise. The significance of these vows lies in their depth and the serious promise they represent, which is intended to withstand the trials of time and adversity.

Another powerful vow or declaration often made is, "for better, for worse; for richer, for poorer; in sickness and in health." It's crucial to note that this vow encompasses both the good and the bad, acknowledging that every relationship will face its own unique challenges. Unfortunately, in today's society, many people who make this vow do not keep it. When faced with difficult times, they often choose to walk away from the relationship rather than work through the hardships.

What they fail to realize is that enduring and overcoming the bad times is what fortifies us and allows us to cherish the good times even more. It's the negatives that make the positives meaningful and worthwhile. Consider the engineering marvels around us: the plane that soars through the sky, the ship that navigates the vast ocean, and the skyscraper that reaches towards the heavens. All these feats are perfect examples of overcoming numerous challenges and adversities to produce the positive results we enjoy today.

In relationships, just as in these engineering feats, it is the obstacles we face and conquer that build the foundation for lasting joy and fulfillment. By embracing the full spectrum of experiences, both positive and negative, we can create a bond that is resilient and enduring. And when we make the conscious choice to fulfill our marriage vows, we open ourselves up to a love that is deeper and more meaningful than we could have ever imagined.

So the next time you're tempted to give up on your marriage during difficult times, remember the power of your vows. Remember that "for better or for worse" means just that - through all the ups and downs, joys and struggles. And by staying true to these promises, you not only honor your commitment but also strengthen the very foundation of your relationship. In doing so, you create a love story that will stand the test of time and inspire others along the way. So never give up on your marriage, for true love endures all things and triumphs in the face of adversity. Instead, hold on tight to your vows and keep fighting for the relationship that you have built together - for it is truly worth it in the end.

In conclusion, while it may be tempting to walk away from a difficult marriage, remember that true love requires endurance and perseverance through both good times and bad. By facing challenges head-on and staying committed to our vows, we can build a bond that is unbreakable and withstands the test of time. So let us strive to always honor and cherish our marriages, for they are a reflection of the greatest engineering feat of all - the human heart. So let us continue to build strong and lasting relationships, knowing that it is through overcoming obstacles that we can create something truly beautiful and enduring. Remember that true love never gives up, but instead finds strength in the face of adversity. Let your marriage be a testament to this kind of love, one that inspires others and stands as a shining example of what is possible when two people come together in commitment and devotion. Together, may we build bridges that connect hearts and withstand the test of time - for there is truly no greater love story than that of a strong and enduring marriage. So let us continue to write our own love stories, filled with challenges, growth, and ultimately triumph - for it is in these tales that we discover the true power and beauty of love. And may each chapter be written with unwavering commitment, endless devotion, and unbreakable bonds - for this is the essence of a lasting and fulfilling marriage. So never give up on your marriage, for true love endures all things and triumphs in the face of adversity. Instead, hold on tight to your vows and keep fighting for the relationship that you have built together. For in the end, it is not the challenges that define our marriages, but how we choose to face them and grow stronger as a couple. So let us remember to always put love first, and with perseverance and determination, we can create a love story that will last a lifetime. Let us continue to write our own tales of enduring love - ones that will be passed down for generations to come. And may we never forget the power of true love and its ability to conquer all obstacles, creating lasting bonds that withstand the test of time.

As we journey through life with our partners by our side, let us always remember the beauty and strength of our marriages. Let us cherish every moment, both the highs and lows, for they all contribute to our love stories. And let us never take each other for granted, but instead nurture and grow our love with each passing day.

Through all the ups and downs, may we always hold on tight to our commitment to one another. May we continue to communicate openly and honestly, always striving to understand each other's perspectives. And in times of conflict, may we come together in love and find a way to overcome any challenges that come our way.

The negative aspects are our imperfections that we bring to the relationship; the negatives that now begin to show up. Initially, everything seems perfect, but as time goes on, these imperfections become more apparent. But after a while, we begin to become more comfortable with each other. Our guard is now down. We are no longer naked and afraid with each other, and this newfound comfort allows us to see each other's true selves.

If we want to avoid jumping from one relationship to another friendship, going from one problem to another, we should pray for grace and wisdom for it. Grace is the long-suffering or patience that leads you to know how to deal with each other, which is wisdom. That's to say that Grace catapults you to your wisdom, and you need wisdom to navigate through your relationship. Navigating through a relationship isn't always easy, it requires the ability to communicate effectively and the willingness to forgive each other's shortcomings.

Always remember that the two of you are the only ones in the middle of the ocean. If the two of you wouldn't like to sink or get drowned, you should try to work out your marriage, not walk out of it. That's the way to survive marriage's storm in the center of the ocean. Just imagine both of you having each other's lives in your hands, relying on each other for support and companionship. This metaphor underscores the importance of mutual effort and understanding in keeping the relationship afloat.

Don't spend that huge amount of money and energy planning

for your wedding, only for you to settle for a mistress with someone that you used to be best friends with. Avoid that lifestyle. It's easy to get caught up in the excitement of a wedding, but the real work begins after the ceremony when the honeymoon phase fades and real life sets in.

It's in the nature of humans to want something new, especially when the old is giving problems. But you don't have to do so. All you need to do to make the old become new is to spice it up and make it new. Everything you are tempted to get new was someone's old stuff, no matter how you try to make it new. That man or woman out there that you want to establish another relationship with at the expense of your spouse at home might not be the best for you. You might just be carried away by their outward nature, but I tell you the truth, you don't really know them. Spice up your own marriage and avoid the ugly experience of becoming the mistress.

In addition, consider the emotional and psychological toll that ending one relationship and starting another can have. The excitement of a new relationship can be intoxicating, but it is often short-lived. True, lasting happiness comes from dealing with issues head-on and finding ways to rekindle the passion and connection with your current partner. Remember, the grass isn't always greener on the other side; sometimes you just need to water your own lawn.

Moreover, think about the consequences of your actions. Not only will you be causing pain and hurt to your current partner, but you may also be setting a negative example for any children involved. Your actions have ripple effects that extend beyond just yourself and your own happiness. Is it worth risking all of this for a temporary thrill?

Instead of looking for something new outside of your marriage, try to find new ways to connect with your spouse. Communicate openly and honestly about your needs and desires, and work together to address any issues in the relationship. Plan fun activities or surprise each other with simple gestures of love and appreciation. Keep the romance alive, and you may just find that there was never a need to look elsewhere in the first place.

Lastly, remember that cheating is not the solution to a struggling marriage. It is important to address any underlying issues and seek professional help if needed. A healthy and happy relationship takes effort and commitment from both partners, but the rewards are immeasurable. Don't give up on your marriage without giving it your all and exhausting all possible options for improvement. In the end, you will be glad that you chose to work on your relationship instead of seeking temporary pleasure outside of it.

So before making any impulsive decisions, think about the importance of your marriage and the love you share with your partner. Don't let momentary temptations cloud your judgment and potentially destroy something that is truly valuable. Remember, true commitment means staying loyal even when times get tough. Keep working on your relationship and nurturing the love between you and your partner, and you will see just how rewarding it can be in the long run.

In conclusion, while it may be tempting to seek excitement outside of a long-term relationship, cheating is never worth the consequences. Before acting on any impulses or desires, consider the impact it will have on yourself, your partner, and your relationship. Remember the importance of communication, commitment, and trust in a marriage. And above all else, never underestimate the power of true love and the value of a strong and faithful partnership. So choose to stay committed and devoted to your marriage, and you will reap the rewards of a fulfilling and lasting bond with your significant other. Keep working on building a strong foundation for your relationship and remember that true happiness comes from within, not from external sources or temporary thrills. Always prioritize your marriage and make it a top priority in your life, because at the end of the day, nothing is more valuable than the love and connection you share with your partner.

So take a step back, reconsider your actions, and choose to put in the effort to improve and strengthen your relationship. You will look back on this decision with pride and satisfaction, knowing that you chose to prioritize true love and commitment over short-term gratification. And in the end, your marriage will stand strong and resilient, able to weather any storm that comes its way because of the dedication and hard work you have put into it. So don't give up on your relationship easily, but instead choose to fight for it with all your heart and soul. Because in the end, a happy and loving marriage is one of life's greatest blessings and joys. So cherish it, nurture it, and always make it a priority in your life. Your future self will thank you for it.

The Impact of Cheating on Relationships

Cheating can have devastating effects on both individuals and their relationships. It can shake the very foundation of trust, communication, and commitment that are essential for a healthy partnership. While the initial thrill or excitement of an extramarital affair may seem tempting, the long-term consequences are not worth risking.

Communication is Key

A strong and honest line of communication is crucial in any relationship, especially when it comes to dealing with issues such as cheating. It may be difficult to talk about, but it's important to address the root causes and underlying problems that lead to infidelity. This open and honest communication can help rebuild trust and prevent future lapses in commitment.

Rebuilding Trust

Trust is a vital component of any successful relationship, and once it has been broken through cheating, it takes time and effort to rebuild. The person who cheated must take responsibility for their actions and actively work towards earning back their partner's trust. This may involve being transparent, setting boundaries, and consistently showing through their actions that they are committed to the relationship.

Forgiveness and Healing

Forgiveness is a necessary step in the healing process after infidelity. It allows both individuals to move forward and work towards rebuilding their relationship. However, forgiveness does not mean forgetting or minimizing the pain caused by cheating. It takes time, patience, and effort from both parties to heal and rebuild a stronger bond.

Moving Forward

While it may seem impossible at first, it is possible for a relationship to survive after cheating. However, it requires dedication and commitment from both individuals to do the work necessary for healing and repairing the relationship. This may involve seeking counseling, setting healthy boundaries, and consistently communicating openly and honestly with one another.

Learning from the Experience

Going through the painful experience of cheating can also serve as a valuable lesson for both individuals to learn from. It can highlight areas of the relationship that need improvement and lead to a deeper understanding and appreciation for one another. By acknowledging and addressing these issues, it can help prevent future instances of infidelity.

Conclusion

Cheating is a devastating betrayal in any relationship, but it is possible for couples to work through it and come out stronger on the other side. It requires open communication, trust, forgiveness, and a willingness to learn and grow from the experience. By taking these steps, couples can rebuild their relationship and create a stronger foundation for the future. So if you are struggling with infidelity in your relationship, know that there is hope for healing and reconciliation. With dedication and hard work, it is possible to move forward and create a healthier and happier relationship together.

Overall, it's important to remember that every relationship is unique and what works for one couple may not work for another. It's important to communicate openly with your partner, seek professional help if needed, and prioritize self-care during this difficult time. By facing the challenge of cheating together, couples can come out stronger and more connected than ever before. So don't give up hope - with patience, understanding, and a commitment to each other, it is possible to move past infidelity and rebuild a loving and trusting relationship.

CHAPTER FIVE

PRIDE AND ITS CONSEQUENCES IN RELATIONSHIPS

We all make mistakes in our relationships, even the person who thinks or feels that he or she has been wronged. This shouldn't, therefore, give you—the offended spouse—the right to abuse the person who asks you for forgiveness. Don't ever think that you now have the upper hand in such a relationship as a result of the offense committed against you. This type of behavior gives no room for growth and harmonious existence in your relationship. In fact, harboring pride and resentment can create a toxic environment where misunderstandings and grievances fester, potentially leading to the deterioration of the bond you share.

In most cases, when the spouse who made the mistake begs for mercy and pardon, the offended partner, out of anger and frustration, usually does not give room for forgiveness. The failure of these spouses to forgive when they have the power to do so has led many relationships to crumble, leaving both parties emotionally scarred. The inability to forgive can create a cycle of resentment and bitterness, making it difficult for both individuals to move forward and heal.

The offended partner normally thinks in such situations that jumping out of the relationship would help them not to feel the pain of the wrong done to them, only to discover later that they couldn't find fulfillment where they ran to. It's often in these moments of isolation and reflection that they realize the depth of the connection they abandoned. They begin to understand that the other party had many good intentions and genuinely cared for them. These realizations often come too late, and the regret of having left something they could have forgiven weighs heavily on their conscience.

It's during that time that they recognize they have made a huge mistake by abandoning their partner for something they would have ordinarily forgiven. The realization that they may have thrown away a valuable and loving relationship over a moment of pride and anger can be a profound and painful lesson. This chapter serves as a reminder that pride should never stand in the way of reconciliation and that fostering a forgiving and understanding heart is crucial for the health and longevity of any relationship. As the saying goes, "never let your ego get in the way of giving and receiving love."

Forgiveness is not only beneficial for the relationship but also for personal growth. It allows individuals to let go of negative emotions, heal from past wounds, and move forward with a clean slate. The act of forgiveness requires strength and courage as it involves acknowledging one's own mistakes and shortcomings while choosing to extend grace to another person.

In addition to forgiveness, effective communication is essential for resolving conflicts in a relationship. When issues arise, it's crucial to have open and honest discussions where both parties can express their thoughts and feelings without fear of judgment or criticism. Through effective communication, misunderstandings can be clarified, and compromises can be reached, leading to a stronger and healthier relationship. However, it's important to note that forgiveness and effective communication work both ways. Both parties must be willing to forgive and communicate for the relationship to thrive. It takes two people to make a relationship work, and both must put in the effort to ensure understanding, empathy, and forgiveness are present in their interactions.

In conclusion, this chapter serves as a reminder that pride has no place in relationships. It is crucial to let go of grudges, practice forgiveness, and engage in open and honest communication for the health and longevity of any relationship. By fostering a forgiving and understanding heart, individuals can cultivate a strong foundation built on mutual respect, trust, and love.

Additionally, it's important to continuously work on oneself and strive towards personal growth. Through forgiveness and effective communication, individuals can heal from past hurts, address issues in the present, and prevent future conflicts. Relationships are not perfect, but with the right attitude and effort, they can become sources of joy, support, and fulfillment. So let us remember to always choose love over pride in our relationships – because in the end, it is what truly matters.

Let us also not forget that forgiveness and effective communication are not just important in romantic relationships, but in all types of relationships – whether it be with family, friends, or colleagues. These principles can help to strengthen bonds and create a more harmonious and understanding environment.

So let's make a conscious effort to practice forgiveness and effective communication in all our relationships, to build a happier and more fulfilling life for ourselves and those around us. Remember, love always wins over pride. So let us choose to forgive, communicate openly, and cultivate healthy relationships filled with love, understanding, and growth. Let's break the cycle of holding onto grudges and instead choose to spread love and understanding in all our relationships. Because at the end of the day, it is not about being right or wrong, but about creating a strong and meaningful connection with those we care about. So let us continue to work towards building and maintaining healthy relationships, one step at a time.

But remember, forgiveness is a two-way street – it requires both parties to actively participate in order for true healing and growth to occur. It's important for both individuals involved to take responsibility for their actions and be willing to listen, understand, and forgive. Only then can true forgiveness and reconciliation take place.

Communication is also crucial in any relationship – it allows for both parties to express their feelings, thoughts, and needs openly and honestly. By communicating effectively, we can avoid misunderstandings, conflicts, and hurt feelings. So let's make an effort to actively listen and communicate with love and understanding, rather than with defensiveness or anger.

In conclusion, relationships are a fundamental aspect of our lives and require constant care and attention in order to thrive. Let us continue to choose love over pride, practice forgiveness and effective communication, and strive towards building strong and fulfilling relationships with those around us. Remember, it's never too late to start working towards healthier relationships – the benefits are endless and well worth the effort. So let's make a conscious effort every day to spread love and understanding, starting with ourselves and extending to those we care about. Because when we choose forgiveness and open communication, we not only strengthen our relationships but also create a more loving and compassionate world for everyone. Let us be the change we wish to see in our relationships and in the world. So let's remember that forgiveness is a continuous journey – one that requires patience, compassion, and understanding from both parties involved.

I am reminded of a person whose wife offended him, and he decided to retaliate. He carried out his retaliation with a sense of vindication, thinking it would solve the problem or make him feel better. However, his confession at the end of the day was that his behavior was rather unhelpful and only escalated the situation. He regretted not forgiving his wife sooner and realized that holding onto resentment only caused more harm than good. Today, the two of them are still living together as a couple, having learned valuable lessons about forgiveness and the importance of communication. He has learned to forgive and prioritize their relationship over momentary grievances.

The mistake some of these mistresses made is that while they were married, their single friends were their only companions. They left no room for their married friends or family members to speak into their lives and encourage them to keep holding on, reminding them that things would surely get better with time. They failed to understand that these single friends of theirs couldn't advise them properly because they lacked the firsthand experience of the challenges that come with maintaining a marriage. They didn't know the place of suffering to keep a relationship until it gets better; they didn't know how to hold on through pain and frustration, among other unavoidable challenges of married life.

These women paid the price of listening to the counsel of their single friends when there were many married people out there who could have helped them navigate the complexities of marital life. They are still married, but emotionally single, feeling isolated and disconnected within their own marriages.

The Bible clearly warns us against pride. It is among the sins that God greatly frowns upon. There are many biblical characters we know who rose and fell, simply because of their pride. King Nebuchadnezzar was a clear-cut example of this downfall, as described in Daniel 4:28-32. He was a powerful king who became consumed by his own arrogance, and as a result, he was humbled by God. His story serves as a powerful reminder that pride can lead to one's downfall, and humility is the key to maintaining a healthy and fulfilling life and relationships.

These lessons, drawn from both personal experiences and biblical teachings, underscore the importance of humility, forgiveness, and seeking wise counsel from those who have walked the path before us. In doing so, we can navigate the challenges of life with grace and wisdom. Whether it be in marriage, friendships, or any other relationship, the key to success is humility and a willingness to listen and learn from others. So let us heed the warning against pride and instead choose humility, knowing that it leads to true growth and fulfillment in all aspects of life. So let us always seek out advice from those who have walked before us, humbly recognizing that no matter how successful we may become, there is always more to learn. Let us choose humility over pride, for it is through this humble mindset that we can truly thrive in all areas of our lives. As the saying goes, "Pride comes before the fall," but with humility, we can rise and overcome any challenges that come our way. So let us remain humble in our marriages, friendships, and all relationships, knowing that it is through this attitude that we can truly connect and build strong, lasting connections with those around us.

In conclusion, while isolation and disconnection may seem like inevitable struggles in marriage, there are ways to combat these feelings by practicing humility and seeking wise counsel. Let us remember the warning against pride and instead choose to humbly learn from others and grow in our relationships. By doing so, we can find true fulfillment and connection with our partners, friends, family, and ultimately with ourselves. So let us embrace humility as a key to thriving in all aspects of life. Let us continue to seek wise counsel and approach every situation with an open mind and humble heart, knowing that it is through this mindset that we can truly flourish in our relationships and in life as a whole. May we never forget the importance of humility and its power to bring lasting fulfillment and growth into our lives.

Humility: A Key to Thriving Relationships

Humility is often overlooked or seen as a weakness in today's society where self-promotion and individual success are highly valued. However, in the context of relationships, humility is a key component to not only maintaining but also thriving in them.

The Dangers of Pride

Pride, on the other hand, can be detrimental to any relationship. When we allow pride to consume us, we become closed-minded and resistant to feedback or differing perspectives. This can lead to conflicts and misunderstandings that cause disconnect and strain in our relationships.

Moreover, pride often leads us to focus solely on ourselves and our own needs, disregarding the needs of others. This self-centered mindset stunts growth in relationships as it hinders our ability to empathize, compromise, and communicate effectively.

The Power of Humility

In contrast, humility allows us to be open-minded and receptive to feedback from others. It enables us to see different perspectives and understand the needs of our partner or loved ones. This promotes empathy and understanding, which are essential for healthy relationships.

With humility, we also become more willing to admit our mistakes and apologize when necessary. This not only strengthens trust and communication in a relationship but also shows genuine care and respect for the other person.

Seeking Wise Counsel

Another aspect of practicing humility is seeking wise counsel. No matter how much we think we know or how much experience we have, there is always room for growth and learning. Seeking advice from trusted mentors, friends, or even a therapist can offer valuable insights and help us see things from a different angle.

The Role of Gratitude

Gratitude is also closely tied to humility in relationships. When we are humble, we recognize the contributions and sacrifices of others in our lives. This leads to gratitude and appreciation, which fosters a sense of reciprocity and strengthens the bond between individuals.

Moreover, expressing gratitude towards our loved ones shows

them that they are valued and encourages them to continue investing in the relationship.

The Impact on Personal Growth

Humility not only benefits relationships but also promotes personal growth. It allows us to acknowledge our weaknesses and strive towards self-improvement. By humbly accepting constructive criticism, we can identify areas for growth and make positive changes in ourselves.

In addition, practicing humility helps us become more humble leaders, colleagues, and friends. It cultivates a culture of support and collaboration instead of competition and selfishness.

Conclusion

Humility is a cornerstone of healthy relationships. It allows us to remain open-minded, empathetic, and appreciative, thereby fostering stronger connections and encouraging personal growth. By continually nurturing humility, we can cultivate more rewarding and meaningful relationships. Let us embrace humility and recognize the profound positive impact it can have on our relationships and personal development. So, let us strive to be humble in our interactions and foster stronger, more fulfilling relationships.

All this came upon King Nebuchadnezzar. At the end of twelve months, he walked in the palace of the kingdom of Babylon. The king spoke and said, "Is not this great Babylon, that I have built for the house of the kingdom by the might of my power, and for the honor of my majesty?" While the word was still in the king's mouth, there fell a voice from heaven, saying, "O King Nebuchadnezzar, to thee it is spoken; The kingdom is departed from thee. And they shall drive thee from men, and thy dwelling shall be with the beasts of the field: they shall make thee to eat grass as oxen, and seven times shall pass over thee, until thou know that the most High ruleth in the kingdom of men, and giveth it to whomsoever He will."

King Nebuchadnezzar was humbled by God for boasting about his achievements. His pride led him to believe that it was by his own strength and power that he had achieved such greatness. As a consequence, God made him lose his sanity, and he lived like an animal for seven long years, eating grass like oxen and dwelling with the beasts of the field. During this period, Nebuchadnezzar experienced the harsh reality of being stripped of his power and glory, learning humility the hard way.

However, this period of humbling was not just for punishment but for enlightenment. When his sanity was eventually restored, Nebuchadnezzar learned to praise and honor God, acknowledging that the Most High rules over the kingdom of men and grants it to whomever He wills. He realized that true power and honor come from God alone, and human pride can lead to one's downfall.

Prior to this humbling experience, Nebuchadnezzar was so filled with pride that he arrogantly thought it was by his own might that he achieved victory and built his empire. God's intervention was a means to teach him and all of humanity the dangers of pride. As stated in Job 33:17-18, "in order to turn away from his deed and conceal pride from man, He keeps back his soul from the pit, and his life from perishing by the sword." Through this divine lesson, Nebuchadnezzar came to understand the importance of humility and the ultimate authority of God.

In today's world, it is easy to fall into the trap of pride and believe that our success is solely due to our own efforts. However, like Nebuchadnezzar, we must remember that it is God who grants us the ability and opportunities to achieve greatness. We should always remain humble and give credit where credit is due – to God.

Furthermore, this story also reminds us that no matter how powerful or successful we may become in this world, we are all ultimately subject to the rule of God. He holds the highest authority over all things, including human rulers and kingdoms. This should serve as a warning to those in positions of power and influence, to use their authority wisely and for the greater good.

In addition, this story also teaches us the importance of seeking wisdom and guidance from God rather than relying on our own understanding. Nebuchadnezzar's pride led him to make foolish decisions, but his humbling experience allowed him to gain true wisdom and understanding that comes from God.

Finally, this story serves as a reminder that no matter how far we may stray from God, it is never too late to turn back to Him. Just as Nebuchadnezzar was able to repent and praise God after his humbling experience, we too can find forgiveness and redemption in God's loving arms.

In conclusion, the story of Nebuchadnezzar and his humbling experience teaches us valuable lessons about humility, the ultimate authority of God, seeking wisdom from Him, and the power of repentance. May we always remember these lessons and strive to live a humble life that is pleasing to God. Let us also pray for all those in positions of power and influence, that they may use their authority wisely and according to His will. So let us remain humble before God as He is the one who ultimately deserves all the glory and credit. As Psalm 62:11 says, "Once God has spoken; twice have I heard this: that power belongs to God." So let us always give Him the credit and praise He deserves in all aspects of our lives.

Let us also remember to share these lessons with others, so that they too may be reminded of the importance of humility and seeking God's wisdom in their lives. Through our actions and words, may we be a reflection of God's love and mercy, just as Nebuchadnezzar was transformed by his humbling experience.

In a world that often values pride and self-promotion, let us strive to live as humble servants of God, following in the example of Jesus Christ who humbled himself even unto death on the cross for our salvation. May we always give glory to God in all that we do and say, for He alone is worthy of all praise and honor.

Job 33:17-18 says, "In order to turn away from his deed, and conceal pride from man, He keeps back his soul from the pit, and his life from perishing by the sword.

The problem of man is that we often fail to hear God speaking to us, urging us to run away from pride. Most of the bad decisions we make in our relationships stem from nothing but pride. 1 Peter 5:6 says, "Therefore, humble yourself under the mighty hand, that He may exalt you in due season." Pride demotes man, while humility exalts him.

Humility is a crucial tool we need for whatever we do in life. There are many prideful people getting married today. We counsel people before they get married, discussing the "dos and don'ts" of marriage, the importance of communication, the need for sexual intimacy, and other aspects, but we often neglect to talk about pride. Pride is hidden in the hearts of many people who are getting married today, and it lies in wait, ready to manifest when there is a challenge.

In every relationship, someone must be willing to apologize even when they are right, for the betterment, progress, and endurance of the relationship. The older generation in relationships would tell you about the sacrifices they made, such as going for counseling, praying together, and fighting to stay together, just to ensure that they remained united. They understood the value of commitment and perseverance.

Unfortunately, this generation seems to lack the knowledge and willingness to fight to stay together. They are more inclined to run away from each other during times of challenges. Imagine spending six months planning your wedding, investing thousands of dollars, and incurring debt, only to stay together for a week. The effort and resources invested in the wedding should reflect the commitment to make the marriage work.

We must recognize the importance of humility in our relationships. Without it, pride can easily take root and cause discord. By fostering a humble attitude, we can build stronger, more lasting relationships that withstand the tests of time and adversity. Let us strive to cultivate humility in our hearts and prioritize the well-being of our relationships over our pride. In doing so, we can create a marriage that is built on a solid foundation of love, respect, and humility.

Furthermore, it is crucial to acknowledge that no marriage is perfect. There will be challenges, disagreements, and difficult times. But through effective communication and a willingness to work together as a team, couples can overcome these obstacles and grow stronger in their relationship. It takes effort and compromise from both partners to maintain a healthy and successful marriage.

In addition to this, sexual intimacy should not be overlooked in any marriage. It is an essential aspect of maintaining a strong connection with your partner and keeping the spark alive in the relationship. Couples must prioritize making time for each other and nurturing their physical intimacy to keep the flame burning.

Overall, perseverance is key in any successful marriage. It requires dedication, commitment, and a willingness to work through the tough times together. By prioritizing humility, effective communication, and sexual intimacy, couples can build a strong foundation for their relationship and overcome any challenges that come their way. So let us all strive to cultivate perseverance in our marriages and create lasting love that stands the test of time.

Although it may seem daunting at times, marriage is a beautiful and fulfilling journey that brings two individuals together in love and partnership. It is a constant, evolving process of learning, growing, and adapting to each other's needs and desires.

Therefore, it is important for couples to continue investing in their relationship, even after they have tied the knot. This can include taking time to go on dates, planning surprises for each other, or simply spending quality time together regularly. Keeping the romance alive and making an effort to make each other feel loved and appreciated can help sustain a happy and healthy marriage.

At the same time, it is also crucial to maintain a sense of independence and individuality in a marriage. Each partner should have their own hobbies, interests, and personal goals outside of the relationship. This not only allows for personal growth but also keeps the relationship dynamic and interesting.

In conclusion, perseverance, effective communication, sexual intimacy, and maintaining a sense of independence are all key components of a successful marriage. By continuously working on these aspects, couples can build a strong foundation for their relationship and create a fulfilling partnership that stands the test of time. Let us remember to always prioritize our marriages and never take our partners for granted. After all, true love is worth fighting for every day. So, let's continue to nurture our marriages and create lasting love together. Happy loving!

Never stop growing together

It is said that change is the only constant in life, and this applies to marriage as well. As time passes, individuals grow and evolve, which can also impact their relationship with their partner. Therefore, it is important for couples to never stop growing together.

This can involve actively learning about each other's changing needs, desires, and goals. It may also mean trying new things together or taking on new challenges as a team. By continuously growing and evolving alongside each other, couples can keep their relationship fresh and dynamic.

Practicing forgiveness

No relationship is perfect, and conflicts are bound to arise in any marriage. However, what truly matters is how couples handle these conflicts and the ability to forgive each other.

Forgiveness does not mean forgetting or condoning hurtful actions, but rather choosing to let go of anger and resentment towards one's partner. It requires empathy, understanding, and a willingness to move forward together positively.

Practicing forgiveness can strengthen the bond between partners and create a more harmonious atmosphere within the marriage. It also allows for personal growth and healing within the relationship.

Continuing to prioritize intimacy

Intimacy is an important aspect of a marriage, and it goes beyond just physical intimacy. Maintaining emotional, intellectual, and spiritual connections with your partner is crucial for a healthy relationship.

As the years go by, it can be easy to let other priorities take over and neglect intimacy. However, it is essential to continue making time for each other and finding ways to strengthen the bond between partners.

This could involve regular date nights or simply setting aside quality time each day to talk and connect with one another. Fostering intimacy in a marriage can create a strong foundation for trust, communication, and overall happiness.

Keeping the romance alive

After years of marriage, it's natural for the initial spark and excitement to fade. However, that doesn't mean couples can't keep the romance alive and maintain a deep connection.

Small gestures of love and appreciation can go a long way in keeping the flame burning. This could include leaving love notes for each other, surprising your partner with their favorite meal, or planning spontaneous weekend getaways.

It's also important to continue nurturing attraction towards each other by taking care of oneself physically and mentally. By making an effort to keep the romance alive, couples can reignite passion and strengthen their bond.

Navigating challenges together

Marriage is not always easy, and couples will inevitably face challenges and conflicts. However, it's crucial to approach these hurdles as a team rather than adversaries.

Effective communication, understanding, and compromise are key in navigating challenges together. It's also important to remember that no marriage is perfect, and it's okay to seek outside help from a therapist or counselor if needed.

Through facing and overcoming challenges together, couples can build resilience and strengthen their relationship for the long haul.

You see, sometimes, God would ask you as the head of the family to go and apologize to your wife, even when you are right. It can be a difficult task, but it takes humility to obey God for the betterment of your relationship. This humility is pivotal not just in marriage, but in any significant relationship. Ask any woman who has a long-standing friendship with a man, and she would tell you the countless number of times she has had to humble herself and apologize to her man, even when she felt she was in the right. This willingness to be humble and seek reconciliation is what makes them celebrate many years in relationship.

Pride breeds stubbornness and that's what has caused so many people to divorce. Someone has to humble themselves in marriage for it to work. When there's no humility, there would be separation and war. Look at the lives of those celebrating any year of marriage anniversary and you would discover that humility is not lacking. They understand that if it had not been for the grace of God, things could have turned out very differently. It is through God's grace and the practice of humility that they are able to maintain a loving and enduring relationship.

The glory is to Jesus who keeps all things together, even when they seem to be falling apart. If He has the whole world in His hands, why not put your relationship in His hands and see how beautiful it would become? Jesus wants to have dinner with you. His dinner comes with a lot of healing, intimacy, and restorative effect. Imagine sitting at a table with Jesus, sharing your burdens, your joys, and your concerns, and receiving His peace and wisdom in return. But the enemy would not allow you to enjoy this dinner with Him. The enemy thrives on division, pride, and stubbornness, and will do everything in his power to keep you from experiencing the transformative power of Jesus' love and grace.

In conclusion, humility, guided by faith, is an essential ingredient in any successful relationship. By trusting in Jesus and letting go of pride, you can cultivate a relationship filled with understanding, compassion, and enduring love. So next time you find yourself disagreeing with your partner, take a step back and ask yourself: "What would Jesus do?" Let His example of humility and selflessness guide you in your relationships, and watch as they flourish under the grace and love of God. And always remember, it's not about who is right or wrong, but about honoring and respecting each other as children of God. So let us continue to practice humility in our relationships and see how it can bring harmony, peace, and joy into our lives. Trust in Jesus and let Him transform your relationships for the better. Remember that with God all things are possible, and that includes having a strong, loving, and humble relationship with your partner. So let us strive to always walk in humility and trust in His perfect plan for our relationships. Let us never forget the power of humility in bringing healing, understanding, and lasting love into our lives. And as we continue on this journey of faith together, may we be reminded that true greatness lies not in being right or having power over others, but in humbly serving and loving one another as Christ has shown us. So let us embrace humility in our relationships, knowing that it is through this virtue that we can truly experience the fullness of God's love and grace. So may we always strive to walk humbly with our partners, with each other, and with our Lord Jesus Christ as our ultimate example of true humility and love. And may His love and grace continue to transform and bless all of our relationships, now and forevermore. Amen.

39.The Bible makes it categorically clear that two are better than one in a relationship. Ecclesiastes 4:9-13 states:

"Two are better than one,

Because they have a good reward for their labor.

For if they fall, one will lift up his companion.

But woe to him who is alone when he falls,

For he has no one to help him up.

Again, if two lie down together, they will keep warm;

But how can one be warm alone?

Though one may be overpowered by another, two can withstand him.

And a threefold cord is not quickly broken."

It is far better and easier to walk in pairs than separately in a relationship. Couples achieve much when they are together, supporting and uplifting each other through life's challenges. The partnership offers emotional support, shared responsibilities, and a strengthened bond that can withstand adversity.

However, if they work against each other, how would their needs be met? Conflict and discord can undermine the unity and progress that a couple could otherwise achieve together. It is crucial to maintain harmony and collaboration to fulfill each other's emotional, physical, and spiritual needs.

Remember that it is the bond that existed between you and your spouse before marriage that the devil stays back to watch. Now, he comes back to disrupt it because he doesn't want you to represent the Trinity. The union between a husband and wife is not just a physical and emotional connection, but also a spiritual one that mirrors the unity of the Holy Trinity. By fostering a loving and supportive relationship, couples can resist external negative forces that seek to create division and strife. Strengthening this bond requires effort, communication, and mutual respect, ensuring that the relationship remains resilient and fulfilling.

It is also important to note that no relationship is perfect; each one has its challenges. But it is how couples handle these challenges together that determines the strength and longevity of the bond. Through open communication, forgiveness, and understanding, couples can overcome obstacles and emerge even stronger.

In conclusion, walking through life with a partner who shares your goals and values brings immense joy, support, and fulfillment. By nurturing a loving and supportive relationship, couples can weather any storm and achieve great things together. Remember, "a threefold cord is not quickly broken." So hold on to each other and journey through life's highs and lows together, united in love and faith.

Let your marriage be a reflection of the unity and love within the Holy Trinity, and you will experience a bond that is unbreakable. So continue to invest in your relationship, communicate openly and honestly, and always prioritize each other's needs. Your marriage is sacred, and by working together as a team, you can overcome any obstacle and achieve true happiness. Therefore, make a conscious effort every day to strengthen your bond with your spouse and build a lasting union filled with love, respect, and harmony. This is the key to a successful and fulfilling marriage that mirrors the love and unity of the Holy Trinity.

Additional Content:

One important aspect of maintaining a strong bond in marriage is having shared interests and hobbies. While it's not necessary for couples to have all the same interests, finding common ground and engaging in activities together can help strengthen the connection between partners.

Another crucial factor in a successful marriage is being able to compromise and work together as a team. This means respecting each other's opinions, making joint decisions, and supporting each other through challenges.

It's also essential for couples to continue to nurture their individual selves within the relationship. This means pursuing personal goals and passions while still prioritizing the needs of the marriage.

Finally, remember that no relationship is perfect, and there will be ups and downs. The key to a happy marriage is not avoiding conflict but learning how to effectively communicate and resolve conflicts in a healthy manner. By doing so, you can grow stronger as a couple and deepen your bond even further. So continue to put effort into your marriage every day, and together with the love of the Holy Trinity, you can create a beautiful union that will last a lifetime. So always remember: "Though one may be overpowered, two can defend themselves." (Ecclesiastes 4:12)

Instead, we should always strive towards growth and improvement in our relationships, especially with our spouse. This can involve constantly learning new ways to communicate effectively, finding new ways to strengthen our bond, and actively working towards maintaining a healthy and happy marriage.

Furthermore, it's important for couples to prioritize not only their physical relationship but also their emotional and spiritual connection. This can include spending quality time together, expressing gratitude and appreciation for one another, and growing in faith together.

Marriage is a journey that requires constant effort, but the rewards are immeasurable. As Christians, we believe that God designed marriage to be a sacred and lifelong commitment. By prioritizing our relationship with God and incorporating His teachings into our marriage, we can create a strong foundation for our union.

In summary, a happy and successful Christian marriage is built on love, mutual respect, teamwork, personal growth, effective communication, and a strong connection with God. So continue to put effort into your marriage every day and remember to never stop learning how to become better partners for each other. With God at the center, your marriage can truly flourish and become a beautiful reflection of His love. So let us always remember to love one another as He loves us and trust in Him to guide us on our journey together.

May God bless and strengthen all marriages, and may we continue to build strong bonds with our spouses through His grace and guidance. Amen. So let us strive towards creating happy, fulfilled, and Christ-centered marriages that bring glory to God. Let us also be a witness of His love through our relationships, inspiring others to do the same. As it is written in Colossians 3:14, "And over all these virtues put on love, which binds them all together in perfect unity." So let us continue to prioritize our marriages and strive towards a strong and loving union with the guidance of God's word. Together, we can build a thriving and enduring marriage that will stand the test of time. As Psalm 127:1 says, "Unless the Lord builds the house, the builders labor in vain." Let us trust in God to be the foundation of our marriage and allow His love to guide us every step of the way.

Remember, marriage is a beautiful gift from God, and with His help, we can create a happy, fulfilling, and successful union that will last a lifetime. So let us continue to nurture and grow our marriages by following the principles of love, respect, communication, and faith in God. And may our marriages be a shining example of His unconditional love for all to see. Let us never forget the importance of putting God at the center of our marriage and seeking His guidance in all aspects of it. By doing so, we can experience true joy, peace, and contentment in our relationship with each other.

In conclusion, building a strong Christian marriage takes effort, dedication, and most importantly, a reliance on God's grace. But with His help, we can overcome any challenge and build a solid foundation for our marriage that will withstand the test of time. So let us continue to strive towards building a strong and Christ-centered marriage that brings glory to God and inspires others to do the same. And may He always be at the center of our union, guiding us towards a lifetime of love, happiness, and fulfillment together. Amen.

As Christians, we are called to honor God in all aspects of our lives, including our marriages. Let us never forget the importance of putting Him first in our relationship and seeking His will above all else. By doing so, we can experience the true beauty and purpose of marriage as it was intended by God.

In addition to putting God at the center of our marriage, it is also important for us to continuously work on ourselves and strive towards becoming the best version of ourselves for our spouse. This means constantly growing and learning together, communicating effectively, and showing love and respect towards each other. As Proverbs 27:17 says, "As iron sharpens iron, so one person sharpens another." Let us never stop sharpening each other through our love and commitment to our marriage.

And as we navigate through the ups and downs of married life, let us always remember to pray for each other, seek wise counsel from trusted mentors or pastors, and never give up on each other. With God at the center of our marriage and a strong foundation built on love, trust, and faithfulness, we can overcome any obstacle that comes our way.

In the end, a strong Christian marriage is not just about two people coming together in matrimony; it is a beautiful partnership with God leading the way. So let us continue to grow in love and commitment towards each other and towards God, as we create a marriage that is a reflection of His love and grace. May our union be a testimony to others of the power and beauty of God's design for marriage. So let us continue to seek His guidance in our journey together and trust in His perfect plan for our lives.

Furthermore, cultivating a strong Christian marriage involves placing God at the center, continuously striving for personal growth, seeking wise counsel, and steadfastly supporting each other. It is a beautiful partnership, guided by Him, leading us towards a lifetime of love and fulfillment. Let us always remember that with God at the forefront, our bond will flourish. We must also keep in mind that communication is vital in any relationship, and it becomes even more crucial in a marriage. Effective communication involves actively listening to each other, expressing our needs and concerns calmly and respectfully, and finding solutions together.

As we face challenges and conflicts, let us remember to approach them with love and respect towards each other. Ephesians 4:2-3 reminds us to "be completely humble and gentle; be patient, bearing with one another in love. Make every effort to keep the unity of the Spirit through the bond of peace." Let us strive to have open hearts and minds as we work through disagreements and strive for unity in our marriage.

Additionally, a strong Christian marriage also involves continuously learning and growing together. This can include reading books or attending marriage workshops and conferences to gain new insights and perspectives on our relationship. It is also essential to regularly pray and study God's Word together, allowing Him to guide us in our journey as a couple.

Moreover, seeking wise counsel from trusted mentors or couples who have walked the path of marriage before us can be invaluable.

They can offer guidance, support, and advice based on their own experiences and knowledge of God's principles for a successful marriage.

Lastly, let us always remember that marriage is a partnership, with both individuals equally contributing and working towards a shared goal. This includes sharing household responsibilities, making decisions together, and supporting each other's personal growth and dreams. As we strive for unity in our relationship, let us keep Jesus as the cornerstone of our marriage and trust in His grace to guide us through every season.

In conclusion, a Christ-centered marriage requires intentional effort from both partners to continuously strengthen their bond with God at the center. By prioritizing communication, love, respect, learning and growing together, seeking wise counsel and embracing partnership, we can build a strong foundation for a lifetime of love and commitment. Let us always remember that with God at the center, our marriage can weather any storm and grow stronger every day. So let us commit to living out His love in our relationship, allowing it to be a testimony of His goodness and faithfulness to those around us. As we do this, we can experience the true beauty and joy of a Christ-centered marriage, reflecting God's perfect love for His people. So let us continue to strive towards unity, growth, and partnership in our marriages as we trust in the Lord's guidance and grace.

Let us never underestimate the power of prayer in our marriage.

Through prayer, we can seek God's wisdom and guidance, ask for strength to overcome challenges, and express our gratitude for the blessings in our relationship. As we pray together as a couple, we invite God into every aspect of our marriage and allow Him to work in miraculous ways.

As we journey through marriage, let us also remember to show grace towards each other. We are all imperfect beings, but God's love is perfect and covers a multitude of sins. Let us learn to forgive each other and extend grace just as Christ has forgiven us.

Finally, let us always keep in mind that our ultimate goal in marriage is not just for our own happiness, but to glorify God and fulfill His purposes. As we submit to His will and follow His plan, we can experience a marriage that is truly fulfilling and meaningful. May our marriages be a reflection of God's love, grace, and faithfulness to the world.

Also, we most never forget the importance of having God at the center of our marriages. With Him as our foundation, we can build a strong and lasting relationship with our spouse that brings joy, peace, and fulfillment. Let us continuously strive towards unity, growth, partnership, prayer, grace, and ultimately glorifying God in our marriages. May our love for each other be a reflection of God's perfect and unconditional love for us. So let us continue to seek Him, trust in Him, and follow His example as we navigate through the beautiful journey of marriage.

40.Fighting and backbiting against each other introduces or

squeezes the devil out of dinner, out of your bed, out of your conversation and in other areas of your life. Just imagine having dinner with Jesus! How would you act? Would you be on your best behavior? Would you make sure everything goes well, ensuring that every word and action is considered? Just imagine how well we would be if that is the way we act with our invisible God. Life would be better for our relationship. "How would this be when you leave the table?" It would just be healing, deliverance and unity. Having a healthy relationship goes a long way. It breeds a healthy way of thinking, even in the way you act. There's no stress, just calmness and easiness with each other. But the enemy does not want it to be so.

Just like you have to cultivate your garden, we get out of our relationship what we put in. Maintaining this level of dedication and effort requires patience and continuous effort. Though, that's easier said than done. It's working hand in hand with our spouse that produces good results in relationships, but the spirit of mistress is against this. The spirit of the mistress occurs when the king got demoted, and now becomes the servant. It's a subtle shift that can gradually degrade the foundation of the relationship if not addressed promptly.

It's time to take that spirit off your life because you are gifted. You are already trained and know how to handle who you were. Get ready to start again, don't settle for less when you have the best. You already have the wisdom, knowledge and understanding and won't make the mistake you made again. Equipped with this renewed perspective, you can approach your relationships with a sense of purpose and clarity, ensuring they thrive and flourish.

Remember, it's not just about you and your spouse, but also about the generations that will come after you. Your relationship is the foundation of your family, and it's important to lay a strong and healthy one for the future generations to build upon. So let go of any negative influences or habits that may be hindering your relationship and embrace a new mindset focused on building lasting love and unity. With God at the center, all things are possible.

Cultivating Healthy Relationships

Relationships play a crucial role in our lives, whether it's with our spouse, family members, friends or even co-workers. They are a source of support, love, and growth. However, maintaining healthy relationships requires dedication and continuous effort.

In today's fast-paced world, it's easy to get caught up in the daily grind and neglect our relationships. We may start taking our loved ones for granted or let negative behaviors creep into our interactions. This is where patience comes in – we must be patient with ourselves and others as we navigate through life together.

But what about when things go wrong? What happens when the dynamic between two people changes, and one person starts acting like a "mistress" instead of a partner? This can happen when we let our ego, insecurities, or past experiences dictate our actions in the relationship. We may try to control the other person, demand things from them, or withhold affection as a form of punishment. In reality, this only leads to further disconnect and damages the relationship.

That's why it's essential to continually cultivate healthy relationships by practicing self-awareness and communication. When conflict arises, take a step back and reflect on your own emotions and behaviors before reacting. Are you projecting your own fears and insecurities onto your partner? Are you truly listening to their perspective?

Effective communication is also key in any relationship. Don't assume that your partner knows what you're thinking or feeling – express yourself clearly and openly. Be willing to listen and understand their point of view, even if you don't agree with it. By communicating effectively, we can avoid misunderstandings and build a deeper level of understanding and trust.

Another important aspect of cultivating healthy relationships is making time for each other. In our busy lives, it's easy to prioritize work or other commitments over spending quality time with our loved ones. However, setting aside dedicated time for each other allows us to connect on a more intimate level and strengthen the bond between us.

Additionally, don't forget to appreciate and show gratitude for your partner. It's easy to take them for granted, but actively acknowledging and appreciating their efforts and qualities can go a long way in maintaining a healthy relationship.

Lastly, remember that relationships are not about power or control – they're about mutual love, respect, and support. By letting go of our ego and insecurities, communicating openly and effectively, making time for each other, and showing appreciation, we can cultivate strong and fulfilling relationships with our partners. And even if challenges arise along the way, by approaching them with empathy and understanding, we can overcome them together. So let's continue to nurture and strengthen our relationships, because at the end of the day, it's all about love and connection. So let's make the effort to prioritize and invest in our relationships, because they are truly worth it. Let's build strong foundations for healthy and fulfilling partnerships that can withstand any obstacles that come our way. Because in the end, what matters most is having someone by our side who loves us unconditionally and supports us through all of life's ups and downs.

Remember, a healthy relationship takes effort from both parties involved. It requires constant maintenance, communication, understanding, and compassion. But with a strong foundation and commitment from both sides, a healthy and fulfilling relationship is possible. So let's continue to prioritize and invest in our relationships, because they are truly one of the most valuable aspects of our lives.

In conclusion, maintaining a strong and healthy relationship requires dedication, effort, communication, appreciation, and understanding. By actively working on these aspects with our partners, we can create deep connections and build fulfilling partnerships that will thrive through any challenges that come our way. Let's never stop nurturing and growing our relationships – because love is worth it all. So let's make sure to take care of ourselves while also taking care of those we love. Let's strive for balance and communicate openly and honestly, so that our relationships can continue to flourish and bring us the happiness and fulfillment we deserve.

Let's also remember to appreciate and cherish the little moments in our relationships, because they are often the ones that hold the most meaning and memories. And when faced with conflicts or challenges, let's approach them with empathy, understanding, and a willingness to work through them together. By doing so, we can strengthen our relationships even further and create deeper bonds of love and connection.

If you had made the mistake before, remember it was as a result of the character you had in the first position, which was caused by ignorance. Now, you have learned from your own mistake and the second chance will be the best. You must be delivered from the spirit of mistress. Ecclesiastes 10:7 says, "I have seen servants upon horses, and princes walking as servants upon the earth." The servant spirit is to serve, while that of the princess is to delegate duties. They are two people but now in wrong positions. As we see, they continue to act in a dysfunctional way. The princess is now in front of the chariot, when she's studied and known all for that position, while the servant who has done and known nothing for the position is on the chariot.

It's time for a switch; it's time to put things into proper order and take back your position in the physical and spiritual. God has given you the authority, walk in it. It's time to take back the first position and be delivered from the stronghold of the mistress, which is settling for the less when you are the best. Isaiah 4:1 says, "And in that day seven women shall take hold of one man, saying, We will eat our own bread, and wear our own apparel: only let us be called by thy name, to take away our reproach."

The Bible in the above verse is talking about the time when the spirit of mistress would become the norm. And that time is already here with us, but you don't have to be a part of that dysfunctional norm. We live in an era where various distractions and societal norms can cause us to stray away from our true purpose and potential. It's crucial to stay grounded in your faith and purpose, understanding that the roles and positions we hold are significant and ordained.

When we recognize our true worth and potential, it becomes easier to reject the notion of settling for less. We must strive to walk in the victory and authority that has been granted to us. This way, we can navigate through life with a clearer vision and a determined spirit to reclaim our rightful position. The power of self-awareness and spiritual awakening cannot be understated. Embrace this moment of revelation and allow it to propel you towards a future where you are aligned with your divine purpose and destiny. Remember, you are created for greatness, and settling for anything less would be an insult to the purpose and potential that God has placed within you.

So take back your position as the head and not the tail. Walk in confidence knowing that you are a conqueror through Christ Jesus. Reclaim your authority and reject any form of mistress spirit that may be trying to hold you captive. You deserve to live a life of abundance and fulfillment, so don't settle for anything less than what God has destined for you. Let go of insecurities, fears, and doubts; instead, focus on your faith and trust in God's plan for your life.

In conclusion, always remember that you are a child of God and have been created with a specific purpose in mind. Reject the idea of settling for less and embrace your true worth and potential. Walk in victory and authority, knowing that God has already ordained greatness for your life. Keep your faith strong, stay connected to your purpose, and watch as you begin to live a life filled with fulfillment, abundance, and divine blessings. Stay empowered and keep living above the norm! So go forth confidently into this world knowing that you are called to be different and make an impact on those around you. Never settle for the status quo, but always strive for greatness and be a shining light in this world. Keep pressing forward towards your purpose and destiny, knowing that with God all things are possible. And remember, as you reclaim your rightful position, also uplift and empower those around you to do the same. Together, we can create a world filled with individuals living in alignment with their true purpose and potential. So let us continue to walk boldly in our calling and make a positive impact on this world. The possibilities are endless when we embrace our true identity as children of God. Don't wait any longer; reclaim your rightful position today and live your life to the fullest! The journey may not always be easy, but with God by our side, we can overcome any obstacle and fulfill our true destiny. Let's rise up and make a difference. So let us go forth in confidence, knowing that we are children of God called to do great things in this world. We have been equipped with all the tools we need to succeed and impact others positively. As we continue on this journey, let us remember to stay connected to our faith, trust in God's plan for our lives, and never settle for less than what we are destined for. Keep shining your light and inspiring others to do the same. The ripple effect of our actions can create a powerful wave of change in this world. So let us embrace our true calling and live a life filled with abundance, purpose, and divine blessings. This is just the beginning of an amazing journey towards reclaiming our rightful position as children of God. Let's continue to push forward, never giving up on our dreams and always staying connected to our faith. With God by our side, we are unstoppable.

As we continue to walk confidently in our calling, we may face challenges along the way. But these obstacles should not discourage us, for we have a God who is always with us and will never leave our side. He will guide us through the tough times and lead us to victory. Let us trust in His plan for our lives, knowing that it is greater than anything we could ever imagine. And in those moments when we feel weak or unsure, let us remember that we are not just ordinary beings, but children of the Most High God.

Let us also take time to encourage and uplift others on their own journey of reclaiming their identity as children of God. We all need support and love along the way, so let's be a source of strength and inspiration for one another. Together, we can make a positive impact in this world and fulfill our purpose in life.

In conclusion, as we continue to embrace our true identity as children of God, let us always remember that with faith, anything is possible. Let us trust in God's plan for our lives, stay connected to Him through prayer and His word, and never settle for less than what we are destined for. May we all continue to shine our light and inspire others on this amazing journey towards reclaiming our rightful position as children of the Most High God. So let's keep moving forward with confidence, for the best is yet to come. Let's keep shining and spreading love, for we are children of God. And that is something worth celebrating every single day. Keep holding on to your faith, for it will sustain you through any storm. We are more than conquerors through Him who loves us, and nothing can ever separate us from His love (Romans 8:37-39). So let's continue to claim our identity as children of God and live our lives with purpose, knowing that we are cherished and loved by our Heavenly Father.

We may stumble and fall at times, but with God's grace, we can always rise and keep moving forward. So let's embrace our true identity, stand firm in our faith, and be a shining example of God's love to the world. May we never forget who we truly are - beloved children of the Most High God. Amen.

And so, as we continue on this journey of reclaiming our identity, may we always remember that God has great plans for us and He will never leave nor forsake us (Deuteronomy 31:6). Let us trust in

His perfect timing and purpose for our lives and have faith that He is working all things together for our good (Romans 8:28). Let's keep pressing on towards the mark, knowing that our ultimate goal is to be with Him in eternity.

But while we are here on this earth, let us make the most of every opportunity to spread God's love and light. Let's be the hands and feet of Jesus, showing kindness, compassion, and forgiveness to those around us. For in doing so, we reflect the heart of our Heavenly Father and bring glory to His name.

So let us continue to walk confidently in our identity as children of God, trusting in His unfailing love and grace. And may our lives be a testament to His goodness, mercy, and faithfulness.

Remember, we are not alone in this journey. We have each other as brothers and sisters in Christ, and most importantly, we have God by our side every step of the way. So let's lean on each other for support and encouragement, but ultimately let's trust in God's strength and guidance to see us through.

As we close this chapter on reclaiming our identity as children of God, let's continue to seek Him daily through prayer and reading His Word. Let's surrender our fears, doubts, and struggles to Him and allow Him to mold us into the image of His Son, Jesus Christ. For only then can we truly live in the fullness of our identity as beloved children of God. So let's continue to persevere in faith, holding onto the promises of God, and confidently walk towards our eternal inheritance in Him. Amen.

May this journey of reclaiming our identity never end, but rather be a continual process as we grow deeper in our relationship with God and embrace who He has created us to be. Let's always remember that we are His masterpiece, fearfully and wonderfully made for a purpose that only He knows. So let's live out that purpose with joy, love, and light, knowing that we are loved and cherished by our Heavenly Father. Let's go forth and shine as His children, bringing hope and redemption to a broken world. As the apostle Paul writes in Ephesians 2:10 (NLT), "For we are God's masterpiece. He has created us anew in Christ Jesus, so we can do the good things he planned for us long ago." So let us confidently step into all that God has planned for us and be a shining reflection of His love and light to those around us.

42.It's time to be original. It's time to think for yourself, be authentic, and make a difference in your society. The mistress is a stronghold that comes from the devil through low self-esteem, regrets, and depression. It's the spirit that settles for less instead of reaching out for the best and trying something new or different.

I know of a lady who had two men in her life in the same church. She got to know one before her marriage, while the second person is her husband. For reasons I don't know, both of them wanted her, and the woman in question didn't have any issue with that. She didn't know how to let one go; she was comfortable with the two. Both of them even followed her to church. I tried to talk to this lady about the need to let go of one of them, but she didn't agree. At the end of the day, she left the church because of that. This lady in question enjoys a dysfunctional relationship.

It's sad that there are people who choose to live the life of a mistress rather than to live in a legitimate relationship. Even when you try to open their eyes to the reality of their situation, they would choose to run away from you. The life of a mistress often involves secrecy, guilt, and constant conflict, which can take a toll on one's mental and emotional well-being. Rather than enjoying the full benefits of a committed, transparent relationship, they settle for a fragmented and unfulfilling experience.

Anything that you have gotten used to doing wrongly, a day will come when you will be faced with the reality of making the right decision, even for your kids and family. You can't continue to live the life of the mistress, sitting in the back of the bus, instead of taking your seat in the front of the bus. It's important to strive for relationships built on mutual respect, trust, and honesty. By making these choices, you pave the way for a healthier, more fulfilling life for yourself and those you care about. So, don't settle for less than what you deserve.

If you find yourself in a situation where you are the other woman or man, pause and reflect on your actions and decisions. Ask yourself if this is truly what you want for yourself and your future. Remember that every action has consequences, and being the mistress can have negative impacts on not only your own life but also the lives of others involved. It takes courage to break away from toxic relationships, but it's worth it in the end.

Letting go of someone may be difficult, especially when there are emotions involved. But sometimes, it's necessary for our own well-being. Don't let the fear of being alone or starting over hold you back from making the right choice. Believe in yourself and your worth, and trust that there is someone out there who will love and respect you fully.

In conclusion, being a mistress may seem glamorous at first, but it ultimately leads to pain and heartache. It's important to recognize our self-worth and make choices that align with our values and beliefs. Remember that true happiness comes from within, not from external relationships or material possessions. Let go of toxic habits and people, and open yourself up to a healthier and happier future. Always strive to be the best version of yourself, and never settle for anything less than what you deserve. So, take control of your life and choose a path that leads to true happiness and fulfillment. You are capable of breaking free from toxic relationships and creating a brighter future for yourself. Trust in your strength, resilience, and worth, and never forget that you have the power to create the life you truly want. Keep moving forward with confidence, self-love, and determination. The journey may not always be easy, but it will be worth it in the end. Remember: you are worthy of love, respect, and happiness - don't settle for anything less. Keep striving towards a life filled with love, joy, and peace, and never hesitate to walk away from anyone or anything that doesn't serve your best interests. You deserve nothing but the best in life, so choose wisely and always put yourself first. Live a life that you can be proud of, one where you are true to yourself and your values. And most importantly, never forget that you are enough just as you are - flaws and all. Embrace your imperfections and let go of toxic relationships that do not value or appreciate them. Surround yourself with people who love and accept you for who you are, and always remember to love and accept yourself first. You are capable of achieving anything you set your mind to, so never doubt your abilities or worth. Keep growing, learning, and evolving into the best version of yourself, and watch as all aspects of your life fall into place. This is your journey towards true happiness - embrace it with open arms, an open heart, and a deep sense of self-love.

The Power of Self-Worth

In today's fast-paced world, it can be easy to get caught up in external factors that may seem like they define our worth. We often look to others for validation and approval, forgetting that the only true source of our self-worth comes from within.

But the truth is, we are all worthy just as we are – flaws and all. It's important to recognize that our worth does not come from our achievements, looks, or material possessions. Our intrinsic worth is something that cannot be measured or compared to anyone else's.

So how do we tap into this power of self-worth? Firstly, it starts with believing in yourself and trusting your own strength and resilience. It's about recognizing your unique talents and abilities and having confidence in them.

Next, it's crucial to set boundaries and prioritize your own well-being. This means saying no to things that don't align with your values or bring you joy, and surrounding yourself with positive influences.

It's also important to practice self-love and self-care. Take time for yourself, whether it's through meditation, exercise, or indulging in a hobby. Remember that taking care of yourself is not selfish – it's necessary for your overall well-being.

But perhaps most importantly, always remember that you are enough just as you are. Embrace your imperfections and let go of the pressure to be perfect. Surround yourself with people who lift you up and celebrate your uniqueness.

When we fully embrace our self-worth, we are able to navigate life's challenges with confidence and resilience. We no longer seek validation from others because we know our own worth. So let go of comparison, stop seeking external approval, and instead, embrace the power of self-worth – it will lead you towards true happiness.

Celebrate Your Journey

As you continue on your journey towards true happiness, remember to celebrate every step along the way. It may not always be easy, but each experience is an opportunity for growth and learning. Take time to reflect on your progress and acknowledge your accomplishments, no matter how big or small they may seem.

It's also important to surround yourself with positivity and gratitude. Practicing gratitude allows us to appreciate all the good in our lives, even when things may not be going as planned. It shifts our focus from what we lack to what we have, creating a more fulfilling and content outlook on life.

Remember that there is no one way to reach happiness – it's a unique journey for each individual. Embrace your own path and trust the process. And don't forget to celebrate yourself along the way – you are worthy, you are enough, and you deserve happiness.

Prioritize Your Mental Health

In the midst of our busy lives, it's important to prioritize our mental health. Just as we take care of our physical health through exercise and a balanced diet, we must also take care of our mental well-being.

This can include practicing self-care activities such as meditation, journaling, or engaging in hobbies that bring us joy and relaxation. It can also mean seeking professional help when needed – therapy or counseling can be incredibly beneficial for managing stress, anxiety, and other mental health concerns.

Remember that taking care of your mental health is not a sign of weakness, but rather a sign of strength and self-awareness. When we prioritize our well-being, we are better equipped to handle life's challenges and pursue happiness with a clear mind and positive outlook.

Spread Kindness

One of the simplest yet most impactful ways to increase happiness in our own lives is by spreading kindness to others. This can be as small as holding the door open for someone or giving a genuine compliment.

Research has shown that acts of kindness not only make us happier, but also have a ripple effect – inspiring others to pay it forward. So take the time to spread kindness wherever you go – you never know how much of a difference it can make in someone's day.

Cultivate Gratitude

Practicing gratitude is another powerful tool for increasing happiness. Instead of focusing on what we lack, we can shift our perspective to appreciate all the blessings in our lives. This can be done through daily gratitude journaling or simply taking a few moments each day to reflect on what we are thankful for.

By cultivating gratitude, we train our minds to see the positive aspects of life and can better cope with challenges when they arise. It also helps us to realize that happiness is not about having everything we want, but rather being content with what we have.

Pursue Meaning

Finding purpose and meaning in life is essential for long-term happiness. This can mean different things to different people – whether it's through a fulfilling career, volunteering for a cause we're passionate about, or simply spending quality time with loved ones.

By pursuing something that brings us fulfillment and aligns with our values, we are more likely to experience a sense of purpose and satisfaction in life. It also gives us a sense of direction and motivation to keep striving towards our goals.

Conclusion

In conclusion, happiness is not a destination but rather a journey. It's important to remember that it's okay to not always be happy, and to allow ourselves to experience a range of emotions. However, by incorporating these habits into our daily lives, we can cultivate a more positive mindset and ultimately lead happier and more fulfilling lives.

So let's make an effort to prioritize our happiness – because in doing so, we not only benefit ourselves but also those around us. As the saying goes, "Happiness is contagious" – so let's spread it wherever we go.

Keep spreading kindness, cultivating gratitude, and pursuing meaning in your life. And remember, the key to happiness is within ourselves – let's unlock it and embrace it every day.

Thank you for reading this document on the pursuit of happiness.

Wishing you all the best in your journey towards a happier and more fulfilling life.

43.The spirit of the mistress is an emotional feeling that binds you, regardless of your age, color, or education. It forces you to confront your deepest insecurities and rise from the depths of self-doubt to the heights of self-empowerment. This spirit represents a way of thinking in a defeated mind, settling for less and weakness, and not realizing the immense strength you possess. Don't be like the elephant. An elephant is so powerful that it can destroy an entire community, yet it remains tamed because someone controls its mind. The mistress is not legally recognized, but the married person is. The mistress doesn't have full rights in the relationship, but the married person does. The mistress is limited in her influence and standing, whereas the married person is not.

It's time to reclaim your position. This is the right moment for you to transition from being the tail to becoming the head in every area of your life. Just like the prodigal son in the Bible, get up, dust yourself off, and return to your rightful position. Your Father has everything you need in life. You don't have to settle for the least when you are destined for greatness. The prodigal son squandered all his father's resources and lived a life far below his potential until his moment of realization came. Today is your moment of realization. Will you be awakened and come back to your senses today? Victory belongs to you if you make that decision. Today, there's no more room for depression, doubt, fear, and all those things that used to keep you down.

Imagine a life where you harness your inner strength and potential, where you no longer allow the limitations imposed by others to define you. Picture yourself breaking free from the chains of mediocrity, embracing your true worth, and striving for excellence in all you do. You have the power to transform your life, to rise above the challenges, and to claim the victory that is rightfully yours. You are not meant to live in the shadows; you are meant to shine brightly and lead with confidence and grace.

So stand tall, embrace your journey, and take the steps necessary to reclaim your position. Your destiny awaits, and your Father is ready to guide you every step of the way. The time is now to move from a place of limitation to a place of limitless possibilities. You are stronger than you think, and the world needs your unique gifts and talents. Believe in yourself, take action, and watch as your life transforms before your very eyes. Remember, you are destined for greatness, so never settle for anything less. Let your light shine and inspire others to do the same. The world will be a better place because of it.

As you embark on this journey towards reclaiming your position, remember that it won't always be easy. There will be challenges and setbacks along the way, but don't let them discourage you. Every obstacle is an opportunity to grow and become stronger. Keep moving forward with determination and resilience, and you will overcome any hurdle in your path.

But also remember to take care of yourself along the way. Self-care is essential in maintaining your physical, mental, and emotional well-being. Take breaks when needed, practice self-compassion, and surround yourself with positive influences. Remember that your worth is not tied to your achievements or external validation. You are valuable simply because you exist.

Lastly, never forget the power of gratitude. Gratitude allows you to focus on the good in your life and appreciate what you have rather than constantly striving for more. It also helps bring a sense of peace and contentment amidst the chaos of life. So take a moment each day to reflect on all the blessings in your life and give thanks.

In summary, you are meant for greatness. Believe in yourself, take action, and never give up on your dreams. Remember to practice self-care and gratitude along the way, and you will reclaim your place as the powerful and limitless being that you truly are. The world is waiting for you to shine your light, so go out there and make it proud. So keep pushing forward, and never forget that you have everything within you to create the life of your dreams.

Additional tips for reclaiming your power:

- Surround yourself with a supportive community: Having a strong support system can make all the difference in achieving your goals. Find people who uplift and motivate you, and let go of those who bring you down.
- Embrace your mistakes: Instead of beating yourself up over your failures, see them as opportunities for growth. Mistakes are a

natural part of the journey towards success.

- Practice positive self-talk: Our thoughts have a powerful impact on our actions and emotions. Make sure to speak kindly to yourself and replace negative self-talk with empowering statements.
- Set achievable goals: Having clear and attainable goals can help give direction and purpose to your actions. Break them down into smaller steps and celebrate each milestone along the way.
- Find inspiration from others: Look to successful individuals who have overcome challenges and achieved their dreams. Their stories can serve as motivation and guidance for your own journey.
- Trust the process: Reclaiming your power and creating the life you desire takes time, effort, and patience. Trust that everything will fall into place in its own perfect timing.

So go forth with confidence, resilience, and determination. You are capable of achieving anything you set your mind to. Remember to always believe in yourself and never give up on your greatness. The world is waiting for you to shine! #NeverGiveUp #ReclaimYourPower #BelieveInYourself #DreamBig. So embrace the journey, stay true to yourself, and create the life of your dreams. The power is within you.

Let these words be a reminder that no matter what challenges or setbacks you may face, you have the strength and resilience to overcome them and continue moving towards your goals.

Keep pushing forward, keep dreaming big, and most importantly, keep reclaiming your power every single day. You are capable of achieving greatness beyond your wildest imagination. So go out there and make it happen!

Remember to take care of yourself along the way – rest when needed, celebrate your successes, and always remember to give yourself grace. You deserve it all.

With every step you take towards reclaiming your power, you are not only empowering yourself but also inspiring those around you. Your journey can serve as a beacon of hope and motivation for others who may be facing their own challenges. So continue to shine bright and be a force of positive change in the world.

Your potential is limitless and your power is boundless - never let anyone or anything dim your light. Stay true to yourself, keep pushing forward, and trust that everything will fall into place as long as you stay focused on your goals and believe in yourself.

So go forth, reclaim your power, and create the life of your dreams. The world is waiting for you to make your mark and leave a positive impact. Remember, never give up, always believe in yourself, and dream big - the possibilities are endless! #NeverGiveUp #ReclaimYourPower #BelieveInYourself #DreamBig.

Let's talk about determination – it is one of the most powerful qualities that we possess as human beings. It allows us to overcome obstacles and challenges, and achieve things we may have once thought impossible.

But what exactly is determination? It can mean different things to different people, but at its core, determination is the unwavering dedication and perseverance towards a goal or objective. It is the driving force that keeps us going when things get tough.

Determination is not something we are born with – it is a skill that can be developed and strengthened over time. It requires discipline, focus, and a strong mindset. But most importantly, it requires belief in oneself and the willingness to keep pushing forward despite any setbacks or failures.

The journey towards reclaiming your power will undoubtedly require determination. There may be days when you feel like giving up or that your goals are unattainable. But it is during these moments that your determination will truly shine.

So how can you cultivate and harness determination in your own life? *Here are some tips:*

- Set clear and realistic goals for yourself
- Create a plan of action and stick to it
- Surround yourself with positive and supportive people who believe in you
- Stay focused on the end result, but also enjoy the journey along the way
- When faced with challenges, remind yourself why you started and keep pushing forward
- Celebrate small victories along the way to stay motivated

Remember, determination is not just about reaching the end goal – it's about the process and the growth that comes with it. It's about finding your inner strength, resilience, and courage to keep moving forward.

And when you do reach your goal, take a moment to reflect on how far you've come and the determination it took to get there. Use this as fuel for future endeavors and continue to harness your determination in all aspects of life.

In conclusion, determination is a powerful tool that we all possess within ourselves. It can help us overcome challenges, achieve our goals, and ultimately lead us towards self-empowerment. So embrace your determination and let it guide you towards a fulfilling and successful life. Keep pushing forward and never give up on yourself – the possibilities are endless when you have determination on your side. So keep striving, stay determined, and see where it takes you in your journey towards reclaiming your power! Remember, the road may not always be easy, but with determination as your guide, anything is possible. Stay strong and resilient, and trust in yourself and your ability to overcome any obstacle that comes your way. With determination by your side, you are capable of achieving greatness and living a fulfilling life filled with empowerment. So keep pushing forward and let determination be the driving force in your journey towards reclaiming your power. Let it be the fire that ignites within you and propels you towards becoming the best version of yourself.

Keep reminding yourself of your purpose and never lose sight of your goals. And always remember, determination is not about perfection or reaching a specific outcome – it's about the strength and resilience we possess to keep going in the face of adversity. So trust in your determination, celebrate every step of the way, and let it guide you towards living a life filled with passion, purpose, and empowerment. The possibilities are endless when we harness our determination and use it as a tool for growth and self-discovery. So keep pushing forward, stay true to yourself, and let determination be your guiding light in achieving your dreams and reclaiming your power. Remember, you are capable of overcoming any challenge with determination by your side. So embrace it, nurture it, and let it lead you towards a life filled with empowerment and success. The journey may not always be easy, but with determination as your constant companion, you will emerge stronger, wiser, and more empowered than ever before. Keep going – the best is yet to come!

Additional Tips for Harnessing Determination

Surround yourself with positive influences and people who believe in your potential. Their support and encouragement can help fuel your determination and give you the strength to keep pushing forward.

Remember to take breaks and practice self-care along the way. Recharging your mind, body, and spirit is essential for maintaining a strong sense of determination.

Set realistic goals and celebrate each small victory along the way. This will not only boost your motivation but also remind you that every step towards your goal is significant.

Don't be afraid to ask for help when needed. Sometimes, having a support system can make all the difference in staying determined during challenging times.

Practice positive self-talk and affirmations. Remind yourself of your worth, strengths, and capabilities regularly to build self-confidence and maintain a determined mindset.

Lastly, trust in the process and have faith in yourself. Remember that determination is a journey, not a destination. Trust yourself to continue growing and evolving as you work towards your dreams and goals. You are capable, resilient, and powerful – let determination guide you towards living your best life. So keep pushing forward, stay true to yourself, and let determination be your guiding light in achieving your dreams and reclaiming your power! The possibilities are endless when we harness our determination – so embrace it, nurture it, and let it lead you towards a brighter, more fulfilling future. The best is truly yet to come! So keep pushing forward, stay true to yourself, and let determination be your guiding light in achieving your dreams and reclaiming your power! The possibilities are endless when we harness our determination – so embrace it, nurture it, and let it lead you towards a brighter, more fulfilling future. The best is yet to come!

You don't have to settle for the least when you can get the best on your way to the promised land. There's a new arising, which is far greater, that is waiting for you just beyond the horizon. But if you don't reject the norm and step out of your comfort zone, you can't experience anything new or transformative. The chain that held you back is broken off. Everything around you is becoming new, filled with opportunities and possibilities. Embrace this change and move forward with courage and determination. Congratulations on this new chapter in your life!

With determination as your guide, there is no limit to what you can achieve. Don't be afraid of challenges or setbacks – they are simply opportunities for growth and learning. Believe in yourself and trust that you have the strength and resilience to overcome any obstacles that come your way.

Remember, it's not about reaching a final destination, but rather enjoying the journey towards your dreams and goals. Along the way, you will discover new strengths, passions, and potentials within yourself. Embrace these discoveries and let them fuel your determination even further.

And always remember to stay true to yourself. Don't let anyone else's expectations or opinions deter you from pursuing your dreams. You are the only one who knows what truly makes you happy and fulfilled. Let your determination guide you towards a life that is authentically yours.

So don't hold back – grab onto your determination with both hands and let it lead you towards an extraordinary life. The best is yet to come, and with determination by your side, there's no doubt that you will make it happen. So keep pushing forward, stay focused on your goals, and never give up on yourself or your dreams. Your future self will thank you for it. The possibilities are endless when we harness our determination and pursue our dreams with unwavering passion and drive. So don't be afraid to take risks, try new things, and step out of your comfort zone. Your determination will guide you towards success and fulfillment in all aspects of your life.

And never forget to acknowledge and celebrate your progress along the way. Each small step forward is a testament to your courage, resilience, and determination. So give yourself credit for how far you've come, and keep moving forward towards an even brighter future.

In conclusion, determination is a powerful force that can help us overcome any obstacles and achieve our dreams. Embrace it, trust it, and let it guide you towards a life that is truly fulfilling. And remember, the journey may not always be easy, but with determination by your side, anything is possible. So keep pushing forward and never give up on yourself – because you are capable of achieving incredible things. Let your determination be the driving force behind all that you do, and watch as it leads you towards a life filled with purpose, passion, and endless possibilities. Keep dreaming big and stay determined – the best is yet to come! So go out there and live your best life – one that is fueled by determination and guided by your unwavering belief in yourself. You have all the tools you need to make your dreams a reality, so never stop chasing after them. Your determination is what will set you apart and lead you towards a life beyond your wildest imagination. Keep pushing forward and let your determination shine bright. The world is waiting for you to unleash your full potential, so go out there and show it what you're made of. Here's to a life filled with determination, success, and endless possibilities!

#Determination: The Key to Unlocking Your Full Potential

Determination is not just a word – it's a mindset, a way of life, and a powerful force that can help us overcome any obstacles and achieve our dreams. It is the key to unlocking our full potential and living a life that is truly fulfilling.

So what exactly is determination? At its core, determination is the unwavering belief in oneself and the drive to never give up, no matter how difficult things may get. It's the inner fire that keeps us going when all hope seems lost. And it's what separates those who achieve their dreams from those who don't.

But determination isn't something that we are born with – it's a quality that we must cultivate and nurture. It requires hard work, dedication, and a strong mindset. Here are some ways to cultivate determination in your life:

◊ 1. Set Clear Goals

The first step towards achieving anything is to have a clear goal in mind. Setting specific, achievable goals gives us something to strive for and helps us stay focused on our journey. When we have a clear goal, we can break it down into smaller steps and create a roadmap towards success.

◊ 2. Embrace Failure

Failure is an inevitable part of any journey towards success. Instead of seeing it as a setback, embrace failure as a learning opportunity. Every failure brings with it valuable lessons that can help us grow and become stronger. Remember, the only way to truly fail is to give up.

◊ 3. Surround Yourself with Positive Influences

The people we surround ourselves with have a huge impact on our mindset and determination. It's important to surround ourselves with positive influences – people who believe in us, support us, and inspire us to be better. These individuals can provide encouragement and motivation when we need it the most.

◊ 4. Practice Self-Discipline

Self-discipline is crucial for cultivating determination. It involves setting aside short-term gratification in pursuit of long-term goals. This means having the willpower to say no to distractions and temptations that may hinder our progress. Practicing self-discipline also helps build resilience, which is essential for achieving our goals in the face of challenges and setbacks.

◊ 5. Celebrate Small Wins

It's important to celebrate even the smallest victories on our journey towards success. These small wins can serve as motivation and fuel our determination to keep going. Don't wait for a big milestone – take time to acknowledge your progress and give yourself credit for your hard work and dedication.

In conclusion, determination is a critical factor in achieving our dreams and goals. By embracing failure, surrounding ourselves with positive influences, practicing self-discipline, and celebrating small wins, we can cultivate a strong sense of determination that will guide us towards success. So never give up, stay focused and determined, and remember that every step forward brings you one step closer to your ultimate goal. Keep pushing through and success will surely follow.

CHAPTER SIX

JOURNEYING BACK TO THE PATH OF RIGHTEOUSNESS.

God's sole plan and purpose is that the backsliders would be reinstated to Him. But the devil is seriously against this and does everything possible to stop it. Just like I stated earlier on in this book, the COVID-19 pandemic has bred many mistresses around the world today. These are people who were once married and dedicated to God; but now, they have become comfortable with being mistresses, living lives that are far from their true calling.

Maybe you have told yourself that you will never become a mistress when you can enjoy the opportunity and privilege of being a married person. However, I sincerely believe that the same people that have backslidden today had the same thought before, just like you do. They once attended church regularly, participated in fellowship, and spent time in prayer and worship. Now, many of them are living beneath their privilege, forgetting their first Love, and their relationship with the Lord Jesus. They have become more engrossed in worldly pursuits, materialism, and the distractions that pull them away from their faith.

Before now, they heard Him knocking at the door of their heart according to Revelation 3:20, but now He's knocking and they are having a hard time opening the door, because they are too busy to entertain Him. Their hearts have become crowded with worries, ambitions, and the noise of everyday life, leaving little room for the voice of the Savior.

Just imagine being busy for the One who saved the best for the last at a wedding in Cana; who restored life back to the prodigal son, and who asked us to bring all our burdens to Him so that He can give us rest. Consider the immense love and sacrifice He demonstrated on the cross, offering us forgiveness and reconciliation with God. It's a tragedy to turn away from such a profound love, to neglect the One who offers us eternal life and peace. Let us remember to realign our hearts and priorities, to make room for the One who deserves our utmost devotion and love. Let us not forget our first Love, for He never forgets us.

As we continue to seek and follow Jesus, let us also remember to be a light and an example to those who have fallen away from the faith. We should never judge or condemn them, but instead show them love, grace, and forgiveness. Let us pray for their hearts to be softened and for them to return to their first Love.

Let us also be vigilant in our own lives, guarding against the distractions of this world that can pull us away from our relationship with God. May we constantly evaluate our priorities and make sure that our love for Him remains steadfast and unwavering.

In the end, it's not about how busy or successful we are in this world, but about our relationship with God and our eternal destiny. Let us choose to open the door of our hearts to Jesus, welcoming Him into every aspect of our lives. And may we never forget the depths of His love for us, always staying close to our first Love – Jesus Christ. So let us make a conscious effort each day to keep Him at the center of our lives, allowing His love to guide and shape us into who He wants us to be. And as we do so, may we also share His love with others, spreading the good news of salvation and leading them to their first Love as well.

Let us never forget the incredible sacrifice that Jesus made for us on the cross, and let us always strive to live our lives in a way that honors and glorifies Him. May His love be our motivation and His grace be our strength as we navigate through this world and strive to follow in His footsteps.

In times of doubt or struggle, let us turn to Jesus as our anchor, knowing that He will never leave us nor forsake us. And when we face difficulties or hardships, may we remember that we serve a God who is greater than any challenge or obstacle we may encounter.

Our first Love, Jesus, has given us the ultimate example of love and sacrifice. Let us follow in His footsteps and live our lives with an unwavering devotion to Him. And as we do so, may we experience the fullness of joy and peace that comes from knowing and loving our first Love – Jesus Christ. So let us hold on tightly to Him, never letting go, and allowing His love to transform us from the inside out.

In conclusion, our relationship with God should always be our top priority. It's not about following a set of rules or fulfilling religious obligations, but about truly knowing and loving our first Love – Jesus Christ. So let us continue to cultivate a deep and intimate relationship with Him, seeking His will and allowing His love to guide our every step. May we never lose sight of the incredible love that God has for us and may it be the driving force in our lives. Let us always keep our first Love at the center of all that we do, bringing glory and honor to His name. So let us boldly proclaim, "I have been crucified with Christ and I no longer live, but Christ lives in me. The life I now live in the body, I live by faith in the Son of God, who loved me and gave himself for me." (Galatians 2:20) So let us continue to love and serve our first Love with all that we are, for He is worthy of all our praise and adoration. Amen.

If you have just discovered your first Love or if you have been walking with Him for many years, may this be a reminder to never take His love for granted. Let us continually seek to know Him more deeply and grow in our relationship with Him. And let us always remember that our first Love will never leave us or forsake us, for His love is unfailing and everlasting. So let us live each day with the knowledge and assurance of God's unending love for us, and may it be the foundation of our lives as we strive to follow in His footsteps. May we be a reflection of His love to those around us, bringing light and hope into a world that desperately needs it. Let us never forget our first Love – Jesus Christ – for He is the source of all love, joy, and peace in our lives.

So let us continue to abide in His love, seeking Him in every moment and allowing His love to transform us from the inside out. And let us always remember that our first Love loves us unconditionally, with a perfect and unfailing love that surpasses all understanding. So let us rejoice and give thanks for this incredible gift of love that we have been given, and may it overflow from our hearts to everyone we encounter.

In the midst of life's trials and challenges, may we find solace, strength, and comfort in the arms of our first Love. And may we never forget that He is always with us, guiding and protecting us through every storm. So let us hold fast to our first Love, and may His love be the anchor that holds us steady through all of life's uncertainties.

As we continue on this journey with our first Love, may we always remember to keep Him at the center of our lives. Let us seek His will above all else and trust in His perfect plan for our lives. And as we do so, may we experience the fullness of joy and peace that comes from knowing and loving our first Love with all that we are. Amen. So let us continue to abide in His love, seeking Him in every moment and allowing His love to transform us from the inside out. And let us always remember that our first Love loves us unconditionally, with a perfect and unfailing love that surpasses all understanding. So let us rejoice and give thanks for this incredible gift of love that we have been given, and may it overflow from our hearts to everyone we encounter.

In the midst of life's trials and challenges, may we find solace, strength, and comfort in the arms of our first Love. And may we never forget that He is always with us, guiding and protecting us through every storm. So let us hold fast to our first Love, and may His love be the anchor that holds us steady through all of life's uncertainties.

As we continue on this journey with our first Love, may we always remember to keep Him at the center of our lives. Let us seek His will above all else and trust in His perfect plan for our lives. And as we do so, may we experience the fullness of joy and peace that comes from knowing and loving our first Love with all that we are.

Let us also remember to share this love with others, spreading light and hope wherever we go. As followers of our first Love, it is our duty to show His love to the world and bring others closer to Him. So let us be vessels of His love, shining bright in a world that desperately needs it.

And finally, may we never take for granted the immense love and grace that our first Love has bestowed upon us. Let us always remain humble and grateful for this precious gift, and use it to bring glory and honor to His name. For He is truly worthy of all our love, adoration, and praise. May we forever abide in our first Love, now and forevermore.

Now, we see empty churches all around the world today. We are experiencing more people who are becoming more religious as the time becomes darker, when we are supposed to be in the church—

the altar of God—crying for our community and seeking divine intervention for the world's troubles. Many people are now at home sleeping, cooking, eating, and doing other things, instead of being fervent for the Lord. Spiritual lethargy and lukewarmness loom around our various churches today. For us the believers, this is not the time for us to be drunk, but to be on the alert and awakened because we still have an adversary who is still the master of deception.

He is a destroyer of our lives; he hates us who are created in the image of God. His schemes are designed to divert our attention from our spiritual duties and commitments. This is not the time to be the mistress, distracted by worldly desires and superficial concerns. Rather, it's the time to be married, fully committed and devoted to our faith. It's the time to take hold of our leadership and recognize who we are in Christ. We are supposed to grab the bull by the horn and realize that we are called to lead and dominate in this world, bringing light to the darkness and hope to the hopeless.

We are not to walk by the world system or to compromise our values and faith principles. The spirit of the mistress will give you the reason to bow to the system of this world, forgetting whose own you are. This spirit wants us to easily forget who we are in Christ Jesus, leading us away from our divine purpose and calling. In Matthew chapter 4, Satan confronted Jesus and asked Him to worship him for the glory and honor that he would give to Him. But Jesus had to remind him where He belonged to, reaffirming His allegiance to the Father. Jesus would never bow to the devil when He is the head, setting an example for us to follow with unwavering faith and commitment.

Now more than ever, we must stand firm in our beliefs, resist the temptations of the world, and remember that our ultimate allegiance is to God. We need to return to our churches, revitalize our spiritual fervor, and lead by example in a world that desperately needs direction and hope. Let's awaken from our spiritual slumber and rise to the occasion, fulfilling the great commission and living out our faith boldly and unapologetically. We must not be afraid to stand out and speak out for what is right, even if it means going against the popular opinions of the world.

As we continue to navigate through uncertain times, let's remember that our faith is not based on circumstances or worldly systems. Our faith is based on an unshakeable foundation rooted in Christ and His teachings. Let's hold fast to this truth and share it with others who may be struggling or searching for meaning in their lives. Let's be bold, courageous, and uncompromising in our walk with God.

In conclusion, although we are living in a time of great challenges and uncertainties, we must not let fear or doubt dictate our actions. Instead, let us remember who we are in Christ and stay true to our divine purpose. Let's be a shining light in a world full of darkness, leading others towards the love and salvation of Jesus Christ. Together, as one body in Christ, we can overcome any obstacle and bring glory to God's name. So let us rise up and proclaim His truth with boldness and confidence, for He is with us always. #EndOfSection

Let us continue to stand firm in our faith, trusting in God's plan and purpose for our lives. May we never waver or compromise our beliefs, but instead hold fast to the truth of His word. Let us also remember to extend grace and love to those around us, showing them the same mercy and forgiveness that was freely given to us by Jesus.

In this ever-changing world, let us not conform to its ways but be transformed by the renewing of our minds through the power of God's word. Let us seek unity within the body of Christ and work towards bringing love and light into a broken world. As we do so, may we be a testament to God's unending love for His creation.

So let us continue to grow in faith, hope, and love, trusting that God is always with us and working all things together for our good. Let us keep our eyes fixed on eternity and the promise of a perfect future with Him. And let us never tire of spreading the message of salvation and hope to those who desperately need it.

In everything we do, may we bring glory to God and fulfill our purpose as followers of Christ. For He is worthy of all praise, honor, and worship. May His name be exalted now and forevermore. Amen.

Let us also remember to keep our focus on Christ, not becoming distracted by the things of this world. Let us prioritize our relationship with Him and seek His will above all else. For only in Him can we find true joy, peace, and fulfillment.

And as we continue to follow Christ and serve Him faithfully, let us never forget the power of prayer. May we constantly be in communication with God, seeking His guidance and direction for our lives. And may we also lift up those around us in prayer, interceding for their needs and standing in the gap for them. For prayer is a powerful tool that can bring about miracles and transform lives.

In conclusion, let us live our lives as reflections of God's love and grace. Let us be agents of change in this world, spreading the good news of Jesus and bringing hope to all those we encounter. And may we always remember that with God by our side, nothing is impossible. So let us continue to press on in our faith journey, knowing that through Him, we can do all things. So let us continue to trust in His plans for us and walk boldly in His purpose for our lives. May God bless us all as we seek to live for Him and bring glory to His name. So let us continue to trust in His plans for us and walk boldly in His purpose for our lives. May God bless us all as we seek to live for Him and bring glory to His name.

In the words of Philippians 1:6, "being confident of this, that he who began a good work in you will carry it on to completion until the day of Christ Jesus." As we continue on our journey with Christ, may we have faith and confidence in His perfect plan for our lives. And may we rest assured that He will never leave us nor forsake us, guiding us every step of the way.

So let us continue to seek Him in all that we do, trusting in His unwavering love and faithfulness. And as we do so, may our lives be a testament to His goodness and grace. Let us never grow weary or lose heart, for He is with us always and His plans for us are greater than we can ever imagine.

In this world full of distractions and chaos, let us hold on to the unchanging truth of God's word and find our strength in Him. For it is through Him that we have been called to be overcomers, to rise above our circumstances and shine His light in the darkness. So let us press on, dear brothers and sisters, knowing that our ultimate victory is already secured through Jesus Christ.

And as we continue to grow in our faith and relationship with God, may we also never forget to extend His love and grace to others. For it is by loving one another that we fulfill the greatest commandment of all - to love God with all our hearts and to love our neighbors as ourselves. Let us be known for our kindness, compassion, and selflessness just as Jesus showed us through His own life.

So let us keep seeking, keep trusting, and keep loving. For in doing so, we bring glory to our Heavenly Father and fulfill His purpose for our lives. May we never stop pursuing a deeper relationship with Him and living out the great commission - to make disciples of all nations. Let us be ambassadors for Christ, spreading His love and truth wherever we go.

This is not the end of our journey but only the beginning. May we continue to grow in faith, hope, and love as we eagerly await the return of our Lord Jesus Christ. And may every moment of our lives be devoted to bringing honor and praise to His holy name. Amen. So let us keep pressing on, dear friends, knowing that God is always with us and His plans for us are greater than we can imagine. Let us never lose heart or grow weary in our pursuit of Him and His purpose for our lives.

In this ever-changing world, may we be rooted in the unchanging truth of God's word and find our strength in Him. For it is through Him that we have been called to be overcomers, to rise above our circumstances and shine His light in the darkness. And as we continue to grow in our faith, may we also never forget the power of prayer and its ability to guide us, comfort us, and bring us closer to God.

So let us keep seeking, keep trusting, and keep loving. For in doing so, we can live a life that reflects the love of our Savior and brings hope to those around us. Let us never underestimate the impact we can have when we surrender ourselves fully to God's will. And may His grace and mercy be upon us as we strive to walk in obedience and follow Him with all our hearts.

As we journey through this life, may we always remember that our true home is in heaven. This world may be filled with trials and tribulations, but our ultimate destination is the everlasting kingdom of God. So let us hold onto this hope and press on, knowing that our labor in the Lord will never be in vain.

In conclusion, let us continue to live as disciples of Christ, sharing His love and truth with the world around us. May we strive to make a positive impact and leave a lasting legacy for His glory. And may we never forget the incredible privilege it is to call ourselves children of God and follow in His footsteps every day. So let us go forth with confidence, knowing that our faithfulness will bring honor to Him and fulfill His purposes for our lives. So let us keep seeking, keep trusting, and keep loving until we are united with our Savior in eternity. Amen. Let this be a reminder to never stop growing in our faith and to always stay rooted in the unchanging truth of God's word.

Let us continue to persevere through any challenges or trials that come our way, knowing that God will never leave us nor forsake us. And may we also remember to extend grace and forgiveness to others as Christ has shown us, for this is how we can truly reflect His love and character.

So whether we are facing mountain-top moments or walking through the valley, let us always fix our eyes on Jesus and trust in His perfect plan for our lives. And may we never forget that we are called to be a light in this world, shining His love and truth wherever we go.

As we continue to grow in our faith and follow God's will, may we also remember to seek community with other believers. Let us encourage and uplift one another, praying for each other and spurring one another on towards love and good deeds.

And finally, let us never lose sight of the ultimate goal - to bring glory and honor to God in all that we do. For in Him, we have purpose and meaning beyond anything this world can offer. So let us continue to live out our faith with boldness and joy, knowing that our ultimate reward is found in Christ alone.

As we conclude this document, may these words serve as a

reminder to always strive for growth in our relationship with God and to never stop seeking His will for our lives. May we walk confidently as children of God, knowing that He is with us every step of the way. Amen. Keep pressing on, my friends. The best is yet to come! #faith #growth #purpose #Godslove #nevergiveup Keep pressing on, my friends. The best is yet to come! #faith #growth #purpose #Godslove #nevergiveup

Keep seeking His truth and walking in obedience, for He has great plans in store for us. May we always remember that our identity is found in Christ, and may we never waver in our trust and love for Him.

So let us continue to live with confidence and boldness, shining the light of Christ wherever we go. And may we always be willing to share the hope and love of Jesus with those around us, no matter the circumstances. For we are called to be His ambassadors and spread His love to a world in need.

In closing, remember that our journey of faith is not meant to be traveled alone. Let us always seek community and fellowship with other believers, and together, let us shine bright for Him who has called us out of darkness into His marvelous light. May our lives truly be a reflection of God's love and truth, as we continue to grow in our faith and serve Him with all that we have. Amen. #faith #fellowship #ambassadorsforChrist Keep shining bright for Jesus! The world needs His light now more than ever. #hope #love #nevergiveup. As we continue to walk in faith, may we never forget the power of God's love and grace in our lives. Let us continue to seek Him with all our heart, and trust that He will guide us on the path of righteousness.

And even when we face challenges and trials, let us hold fast to the promises of God and remember that our ultimate reward is found in Christ alone. For it is through Him that we have eternal life and a home in heaven with our Heavenly Father.

Even in His confrontation, Jesus still stood firm. He gave no room for the enemy to make Him think twice about who He is. We should be imitators of our Lord Jesus! The enemy desires and enjoys our worship. He wants to take the position of God in our lives so that we can worship him. However, it's only those in darkness, who are ruled by ignorance, that worship him as the king of darkness. Many people now worship at the devil's feet; they have now become his mistresses. These are the people who earlier followed God and are familiar with His presence and ways.

To the many mistresses out there, it's high time you came back to your rightful position by repenting and changing your ways. It's time to come back to Jesus, who is the only giver of true joy, peace, and tranquility. The world has nothing to offer you except death and destruction. Come back to His grace and the eternal love that He has for you, rather than subjecting yourself to the yoke of darkness. To the mistress who once knew God, He is saying to you, "Forsake your ways and thoughts and return to Me." It may feel that you can't, but that's just your feeling. Use your will and turn back to Him.

The Bible says in John 8:36 that "whom the Son sets free is free indeed." Choose to be a prisoner of Christ, like Apostle Paul. You are limited when you become a prisoner to the world system; but there's no such limit in becoming a prisoner of Christ. Walk out of darkness into your freedom. The world may promise you fleeting pleasures, but these come at the cost of your soul. Only in Christ will you find lasting fulfillment and purpose.

Remember, Jesus offers a kind of freedom that the world cannot give. His yoke is easy, and His burden is light. He calls you to a life of abundance, not one of bondage. So, heed His call today and walk out of the shadows into the marvelous light He offers. The more you learn and understand His word, the stronger you become in resisting the enemy's attempts to lead you astray. Embrace His promises and let His love guide you back to the path of righteousness.

As you turn away from your past life as a mistress, also find comfort in knowing that God is a loving and forgiving God. Confess your sins and ask for His forgiveness. He is faithful to forgive and cleanse us from all unrighteousness (1 John 1:9). Don't let guilt or shame hold you back from experiencing the freedom and abundant life that Jesus offers.

Additionally, surround yourself with fellow believers who will support and encourage you on your journey. Find a church community where you can grow in your faith and receive guidance from spiritual leaders. Seek out accountability partners who can help keep you accountable in your walk with Christ.

Remember, true freedom comes from surrendering to Jesus and living a life according to His teachings. Don't let the lies of the world hold you captive any longer. Choose to break free from the chains of sin and embrace the abundant life that God has planned for you. Trust in His love and promises, and walk boldly into the freedom that can only be found in Him. So go forth, my sister, as a new creation in Christ and live as a testimony of His transforming power in your life!

No matter what struggles or temptations may come your way, always remember that through Christ, you are more than a conqueror (Romans 8:37). Keep growing in your faith and trust in God's perfect plan for your life. Let His love shine through you and lead others to the same freedom that you have found in Him.

And when doubts or fears arise, simply turn to His word and meditate on the truth of who He is and what He has done for you. You are loved, accepted, forgiven, and redeemed by the blood of Jesus. May this truth continually strengthen and guide you as you embrace your new identity in Christ.

In conclusion, know that as a former mistress, you are not defined by your past mistakes but by the grace and love of God. You have been set free from shame, guilt, and condemnation through Jesus' sacrifice on the cross. Embrace His forgiveness and choose to walk in freedom as a daughter of the Most High God. So continue to seek Him, trust Him, and follow Him wholeheartedly. For it is only through Him that true freedom can be found. May you experience an abundant life filled with joy, peace, and purpose as you journey with Christ. Amen.

This is just the beginning of your new life in Christ! Keep growing in your relationship with Him and allow His love to transform you from the inside out. Never forget the power of His grace and always remember that in Him, you are a new creation. So go forth with confidence, knowing that you are loved, chosen, and called for a purpose. May your life be a testimony of God's amazing love and may others be drawn to know Him through your story. And above all, never cease to give thanks to God for His unending mercy and grace in your life. He has truly rescued you from darkness into His marvelous light (1 Peter 2:9).

So rejoice in this new identity and continue to walk in the freedom that Christ has given you. Your past does not define you, but rather, it serves as a reminder of God's redemptive power in your life. As you journey with Him, may you continuously grow in faith, hope, and love. And remember, you are not alone in this journey – God is with you every step of the way (Isaiah 41:10). So hold onto His promises and trust in His perfect plan for your life. In Him, all things are possible (Matthew 19:26).

So let go of any shame or guilt and fully embrace the abundant life that God has for you. Don't let your past hold you back, but instead, use it as a testimony to bring glory to God and inspire others. And always remember, through Christ, you are more than a conqueror (Romans 8:37). So keep pressing on in faith and never lose sight of the victory that is yours in Him. May His love continue to fill your heart and overflow into every aspect of your life. This is just the beginning of an incredible journey with God – one that will lead to eternal life with Him in heaven. Keep seeking Him, trusting Him, and loving Him with all your heart. And may His love and grace sustain you every step of the way.

As you continue on this journey with God, it is important to surround yourself with a community of believers who will support and encourage you. Find a local church or small group where you can grow in fellowship and accountability. It is through these relationships that we can find strength, guidance, and encouragement to keep walking in faith.

Also remember to stay connected with God through prayer and studying His word. This is how we deepen our relationship with Him and gain understanding of His will for our lives. May the Holy Spirit guide you and give you wisdom as you seek His will and purpose for your life.

Never forget that God has a great plan for your life – one that is filled with hope, joy, and purpose. Embrace every step of the journey and trust in Him to lead you to all He has planned for you. And may the love of Christ be the foundation of everything you do, guiding and sustaining you through every season of life. #continuefaithjourney #trustgod #loveothers

"For I know the plans I have for you," declares the Lord, "plans to prosper you and not to harm you, plans to give you

hope and a future." - Jeremiah 29:11

So keep pressing on in faith, knowing that God is with you every step of the way. And as you continue to grow in your relationship with Him, may His love shine through you and impact those around you for His glory. Let your journey be a testimony of God's goodness and grace, and may it inspire others to seek Him and experience the abundant life He has promised us. Trust in His plan, trust in His timing, and never lose sight of the hope we have in Jesus Christ – our Savior and Lord. #nevergiveup #faithoverfear #hopeinjesus

Let us run with perseverance the race marked out for us, fixing our eyes on Jesus, the pioneer and perfecter of faith. -Hebrews 12:1-2a

So keep running your race and never give up, for God is faithful and He will see you through to the finish line. Stay rooted in His love, His word, and His promises. And may your faith journey continue to be a source of inspiration and growth in your relationship with Him. Amen.

"And let us not grow weary while doing good, for in due season we shall reap if we do not lose heart." - Galatians 6:9

So keep sowing seeds of love, kindness, and faith wherever you go. Trust in God's timing and His plan, for He will bring about a beautiful harvest in your life. And may your journey be marked by perseverance, courage, and unwavering trust in the One who holds all things together. Remember that you are never alone on this journey – God is with you every step of the way. So keep walking in faith, knowing that He has great plans for your life. Don't give up, don't lose hope, and continue to trust in the goodness of our faithful God. #perseverance #trustinthelord #nevergiveup So let us press on, dear friends, with faith and courage as we journey towards our ultimate destination – eternity with our Heavenly Father. May our lives be a living testament of His love and grace, shining brightly for all to see. And may we never forget the power of perseverance and the strength that comes from placing our hope in Jesus Christ. Keep running your race, keep trusting in God's plan, and know that you are loved beyond measure. So let us continue to encourage one another, lift each other up in prayer, and support one another as we run this race together. And may our faith journey be a testimony of God's goodness and faithfulness in our lives. Keep pressing on, dear friends, for the best is yet to come! #faithjourney #nevergiveup #Godisfaithful

Let us also remember that our faith journey is not just about ourselves, but it is also about sharing the love of Christ with others. As we grow in our own relationship with Him, let us also strive to be a light and example to those around us. Let us spread hope, love, and encouragement to those who may be struggling on their own journey. And as we do so, let us always keep our focus on God and trust in His perfect timing and plan for each of our lives.

Furthermore, let us embrace the challenges and trials that come our way, knowing that they are opportunities for growth and refinement. Instead of being discouraged by them, let us lean into God's strength and grace to overcome them. For it is through these difficulties that we become stronger in our faith and closer to Him.

In addition, let us also continue to seek His guidance and direction in our lives, surrendering our plans and desires to Him. For it is only through His perfect will that we can truly fulfill our purpose and reach the full potential He has for us.

And when we face moments of doubt or uncertainty, let us remember the promises of God's word and stand firm on them. Let us declare with confidence that we are more than conquerors through Christ who loves us (Romans 8:37), and that He will never leave us nor forsake us (Deuteronomy 31:6).

As we journey onward, may we always keep our eyes fixed on Jesus and trust in His unfailing love and faithfulness. For He is the author and perfecter of our faith (Hebrews 12:2), and with Him by our side, we can overcome any obstacle that comes our way.

So let us continue to persevere in our faith journey, knowing that in the end, it will all be worth it. And when we reach our final destination in heaven, we will rejoice in God's goodness and grace, for He has been faithful every step of the way. #eternitywithGod #nevergiveup #faithfulGod

May this be an encouragement to all who read, to trust in God's perfect timing and plan for their lives, and to continue pressing on towards the goal of eternal life with Him. For truly, there is no greater joy and fulfillment than living a life surrendered to the Lord.

Let us therefore keep striving towards that ultimate prize, knowing that in His hands, we are always secure and loved beyond measure. #trustGod #eternallife #seekHimfirst

In conclusion, let us remember that God's plan for our lives may not always align with our own plans or desires. But His ways are higher than ours (Isaiah 55:9) and His plans are always for our ultimate good (Jeremiah 29:11). So let us trust in His sovereignty and surrender our lives to Him, knowing that He will guide us towards a purposeful and fulfilling life. Let us continue to seek after Him, follow His word, and rely on His strength every step of the way. For in Him, we can truly live a life without regrets or uncertainties, but one filled with hope, joy and peace that surpasses all understanding. #Godsplan #hopeinHim #trustandobey

So as we journey through this life, let us fix our eyes on Jesus, the author and perfecter of our faith (Hebrews 12:2), and keep running towards the finish line with endurance. For in Him, we have everything we need to live a victorious and purposeful life. And in the end, when we enter into His eternal kingdom, we will hear those sweet words from our Lord and Savior saying, "Well done, good and faithful servant." (Matthew 25:23) Let us continue to hold fast to our faith in Him, for He is faithful till the very end. Amen. #nevergiveup #endure #faithfulservant So let us continue to trust in God, seek after Him, and follow His will for our lives. For in doing so, we will experience true joy, fulfillment and eternal life with Him. May our hearts be always surrendered to His perfect plan for us, and may we never lose sight of the ultimate prize that awaits us in eternity. Let us live each day with purpose and determination, knowing that we are loved by a faithful God who will never leave us nor forsake us (Deuteronomy 31:6). #eternitywithGod #neveralone #lovedbyGod

As we continue to grow and mature in our faith, let us also remember to share the good news of Jesus with others. Let us be bold and unashamed in proclaiming His name, for He is the only way, truth, and life (John 14:6). Let us show love and compassion towards those around us, just as Jesus did during His time on earth. And may our lives be a testimony of God's goodness and grace.

In times of uncertainty and trials, let us turn to God's word for comfort and guidance. For it is through His word that we can find strength, hope, and peace in the midst of any storm. Let us also remember to pray without ceasing (1 Thessalonians 5:17), knowing that our prayers have power and can move mountains (Matthew 17:20).

As we strive to be faithful servants of God, let us also remember to rest in His love and grace. We do not need to earn our salvation or God's love; it is a free gift given to us through Jesus' sacrifice on the cross. Let us never lose sight of this truth and always remember that our identity and worth are found in Him alone.

And finally, let us look forward to the day when we will be reunited with our Heavenly Father in eternity. For as believers, our citizenship is in heaven (Philippians 3:20) and we eagerly await the return of our Savior. Let us live each day with an eternal perspective, knowing that this life on earth is temporary and our true home is with God forever.

So let us continue to follow Jesus wholeheartedly, living a life filled with love, purpose, and hope for the glory of God. And may His kingdom come and His will be done on earth as it is in heaven (Matthew 6:10). Amen.

As we conclude this discussion on living a life devoted to God, let us remember that it is not always easy. We will face challenges and obstacles along the way, but through it all, we can trust in God's faithfulness and love for us.

Let us also remember to surround ourselves with fellow believers who can encourage and uplift us in our journey of faith. We are meant to be part of a community, supporting each other and growing together in our relationship with God.

And as we continue to grow and learn more about God's character and His will for our lives, may we never stop seeking Him and His kingdom above all else. Let us always strive to "move mountains" for God, knowing that with faith and obedience, nothing is impossible (Mark 11:23). May we be a shining light in this world, reflecting the love and goodness of our Heavenly Father to those around us.

The Psalmist says, "if it were not the grace of God, where would I be." This statement serves as a powerful reminder of the boundless grace and mercy that God extends to us every day. Come back to your marriage with God while the grace is still stretching out to you, inviting you to return. The truth is that, at some point, we all have played the role of a mistress, straying from our rightful place. However, we grew weary of that path and decided to embrace our true identity in Christ. Make the same decision today, and you won't regret it. The era of playing the mistress is over in your life. Embrace your new beginning with confidence and faith. Congratulations on this transformative journey!

The grace of God is truly amazing, and it extends beyond just our personal relationship with Him. It also covers our relationships with others, including our marriages. As we strive to grow closer to God, let us also make the effort to strengthen and nurture our marriages.

Marriage is a beautiful gift from God, but it can also face challenges and difficulties. However, we have the assurance that through His grace and love, we can overcome any obstacle in our marriage. Let us not give up on our spouses or ourselves but instead choose to extend grace and forgiveness as God has done for us.

And as we continue to walk in the grace of God, let us also extend this grace to others. Let us be quick to forgive and slow to anger, showing love and compassion just as Jesus did for us. May our marriages be a reflection of God's unconditional love and grace towards His children.

In conclusion, the grace of God is more than sufficient for all our needs, including our marriages. As we surrender ourselves to Him and allow His grace to transform us, we can experience true joy and fulfillment in our relationships with our spouses. So let us continue to walk in His grace and share it with those around us. So that his glory may be known and His love may shine through us. Let us embrace the transformative power of God's grace in our marriages, and watch as He works miracles in our lives. So let us continue to trust in Him and His plans for our marriages, knowing that with His grace, all things are possible. Amen. There is no end to the blessings we can receive when we choose to walk in the grace of God. May we always remember that His grace is enough for every situation, including our marriages, and may we continually strive to extend this grace to others as well.

So let us hold onto God's unending grace in our marriages and trust in His perfect timing. As we do so, we can have confidence that He is working all things together for our good and the strengthening of our relationship with our spouse. And as we continue to seek God's guidance and lean on His grace, may our marriages be a testament to His faithfulness and love.

In all things, let us remember that it is only through God's grace that we can truly thrive in our marriages. So let us cling to this amazing gift from above, allowing it to transform us into better spouses, partners, and individuals. May the grace of God guide us every step of the way, bringing us closer to Him and to each other. And may our marriages be a beautiful reflection of His love and grace for the world to see. As we continue on this journey, let us always remember that with God's grace, our marriages can truly be a source of joy, strength, and blessing in our lives. So let us never stop seeking His grace and allowing it to work wonders in our relationships. For the glory of God and the betterment of our marriages, let us always choose to walk in His amazing grace. Amen. So let us continue to trust in His plan for our marriages and have faith that His grace will sustain us through every trial and triumph. And may we always give thanks for this incredible gift, knowing that with God's grace, all things are possible. Let us live in the fullness of His grace and never forget to extend it to others, especially our spouse. For as we do so, we can experience a marriage filled with love, forgiveness, and true intimacy with both God and each other. So let us hold onto the unending grace of God in our marriages and allow it to transform us into the best version of ourselves. May His grace be ever-present in our lives and marriages, now and forevermore. So let us hold fast to the truth that our God is a God of grace, and His grace is always available to us in every season of our marriage. Let us never hesitate to seek it out, for it is through His grace that we can find true healing, restoration, and renewal in our relationships. And may we always remember that in His unending grace, there is hope for every brokenness and strength for every weakness. Let us allow His grace to guide and sustain our marriages, so that they may continue to be a beautiful testimony of His love and faithfulness in our lives. May we always choose to walk in the light of His grace, and may it overflow into every aspect of our marriage, bringing peace, joy, and fulfillment. So let us never underestimate the power of God's grace in our marriages and continue to seek it with all our hearts. For through His grace, we can truly experience a marriage that reflects the love and beauty of Christ. Let us cling to His grace tightly, hold onto it with all our might, and never let go. And as we do so, may we see how His amazing grace can transform even the most broken relationships into something beautiful and extraordinary. Let us never forget that with God's grace, all things are possible. So let us choose to live in His grace every day and watch as it works wonders in our marriages.

As we journey through life, we will undoubtedly face challenges and struggles within our marriages. But even in the midst of these difficulties, let us remember to always extend grace towards one another, just as God has extended His grace towards us.

Let us also be mindful of the importance of forgiveness in marriage. Just as we have been forgiven by God for our mistakes and shortcomings, so too should we forgive one another in our marriages. Forgiveness is a key component in maintaining a healthy and strong relationship, and it allows us to move forward with love and grace.

Additionally, let us not forget the power of communication in our marriages. Open and honest communication is vital for understanding and strengthening our bond with our spouse. And as we communicate, may we always do so with kindness, love, and grace.

Lastly, let us never stop growing in our marriages. Just as God calls us to continually grow in our faith, so too should we strive to grow individually and together within our marriage. With His grace as our guide, may we always seek to become better spouses, to love and serve one another selflessly, and to honor God in our relationship.

In conclusion, the beauty of Christ's grace is evident not only in our individual lives but also in our marriages. Let us hold onto His grace tightly and allow it to transform and strengthen our relationships as we journey through life together. May we always extend grace, practice forgiveness, communicate with love, and continue growing in our marriages for the glory of God. So let us cling to His grace tightly, hold onto it with all our might, and never let go! Because with His amazing grace, all things are truly possible and our marriages can be a reflection of His boundless love. Let us choose to walk in grace, both individually and in our marriages, every day. Because with God's grace, we can overcome any challenge, heal any wounds, and experience the fullness of joy that comes from living in alignment with His will. So let us continue to seek His grace in our lives and allow it to transform us into better individuals, spouses, and partners for the glory of God.

May we always remember that our marriages are a testament to God's love and faithfulness. And as we journey through life together with our spouse, may we always choose to extend grace towards one another, just as God extends His unending grace and love towards us. For it is through extending grace that we can truly experience the beauty of a Christ-centered marriage filled with love, kindness, forgiveness, and growth. So let us never forget the power of God's grace in our relationships, and may it continue to guide us and strengthen us every day.

In all things, may His grace remain at the center of our marriages, drawing us closer to each other and to Him. And as we navigate through the highs and lows of life together, let us always remember that with God's grace, we can overcome anything and emerge stronger and more united than ever before. So let us continue to seek His grace, hold onto it tightly, and extend it generously towards our spouse as we journey together in this beautiful gift of marriage. With God's grace, we can truly have a marriage that shines for His glory and brings joy and fulfillment to our lives. Let us never stop growing in His grace and love, both individually and as a couple, so that our marriages may be a testament to His goodness and faithfulness until the end of time. So let us always cling to God's amazing grace, for it is the foundation of a truly blessed and fulfilling marriage.

May we never cease to be amazed by the depth of God's grace and love for us. And may we always strive to extend that same grace and love towards our spouse, just as Christ extends it towards us every day. Let us continue to seek His guidance, His strength, and His grace in all aspects of our marriages, so that we may fulfill His purpose for our lives together. For with His grace, anything is possible, and our marriages can truly become a beautiful reflection of His unfailing love. So let us hold onto God's grace tightly, and may it continue to shape and transform our relationships for the better. Amen.

As we journey through life with our spouse, let us not forget to also extend God's grace towards others around us. Let us be a shining example of His love and forgiveness, showing kindness and compassion even in difficult situations. For just as we have received His unmerited grace in our own lives, so should we freely give it to those around us.

In times of conflict or hardship within our marriages, let us remember to lean on God's amazing grace and seek His wisdom and guidance. For only He can soften hardened hearts, heal broken relationships, and bring about true reconciliation. Let us trust in His perfect plan for our marriages, even when things may seem uncertain or difficult.

And finally, let us never forget that God's grace is always sufficient for us. No matter what challenges we may face in our marriages, He has promised to be with us every step of the way. So let us continue to rely on His grace and walk confidently in the knowledge that He is working all things together for our good and His glory. Therefore, let us continually give thanks for His amazing grace and strive to extend it towards others in all areas of our lives, including our marriages. May His grace continue to abound in us and through us, bringing joy, peace, and fulfillment to our marriages. So let us hold onto God's grace tightly, and may it continue to shape and transform our relationships for the better. Amen.

As we journey through life with our spouse, let us not forget to also extend God's grace towards others around us. Let us be a shining example of His love and forgiveness, showing kindness and compassion even in difficult situations. For just as we have received His unmerited grace in our own lives, so should we freely give it to those around us. Let us continue to spread God's grace in our marriages and beyond, being a light in this world and reflecting His goodness and mercy to all those we encounter. So let us continually seek His grace, be transformed by it, and share it with others, for the glory of God and the building up of His kingdom. May our marriages be a testament to His amazing grace, now and always. So let us never grow weary in sharing God's grace with others, knowing that through it all, He is working out His perfect plan for our lives and our relationships. For truly, there is no greater gift than His grace, and may we always remember to extend it towards others, just as He has extended it towards us. Let us keep walking in His grace, with our spouses by our side, trusting in Him every step of the way. Amen.

Grace in Marriage: A Never-Ending Journey

The concept of grace is essential not only in our relationship with God but also within the context of marriage. As we continue to journey through life together with our spouse, let us never forget the significance of extending God's grace towards one another.

In this never-ending journey of marriage, there will be moments where we may stumble and fall, where we may hurt or disappoint our spouse. And in those moments, it is God's grace that sustains us and teaches us to extend the same grace towards our partner.

But extending grace goes beyond just forgiving one another

for our mistakes. It also means showing love and compassion even in difficult situations, choosing to see the best in each other and offering forgiveness instead of holding grudges.

Furthermore, as we receive God's unmerited grace in our own lives, let us be quick to extend it to those around us - whether it be family members, friends, or even strangers. Let us be a beacon of God's love and grace in our marriages, spreading it to others through our actions and words.

And just as God never grows tired of extending His grace towards us, may we also never grow weary in sharing it with our spouse. Let us continually seek God's guidance in our marriage and trust that He is working out His perfect plan for us.

So let us keep walking hand-in-hand with our spouses, journeying through life together, always striving to extend and receive God's amazing grace. For truly, there is no greater gift than His grace, and may it always be the foundation of our marriages - a constant reminder of His love and faithfulness towards us. So let us hold fast to God's grace, both in our relationship with Him and in our marriage, trusting that it will sustain and strengthen us through all the ups and downs of life. And may we always be grateful for the gift of grace that binds us together as one with our spouse and with God.

Let this be our prayer - that we may continue to grow in grace, both individually and as a couple, never ceasing to extend it towards each other and those around us. For where there is grace, there is also love, forgiveness, patience, and all the other qualities that make a strong and lasting marriage. May our marriages be a reflection of God's grace, a testimony to His unending love for us, and a source of hope and inspiration for others.

So let us never forget the power of grace in our marriages - let it be the foundation upon which we build our relationship with each other, always striving to extend it towards one another as God extends it towards us. And may His boundless grace continue to guide us through every season of life, making our marriage stronger, more beautiful, and filled with endless possibilities. So let us keep growing in grace, always seeking to become more like Christ, and allowing His love to flow through us into our marriages and the world around us. With God's grace as our anchor, there is no storm that we cannot weather, no obstacle that we cannot overcome, and no distance too great for us to travel together. So let us hold fast to His grace and journey on towards the perfect plan He has in store for our marriage. Let this be our daily reminder - that with God's grace, all things are possible. So let us continue to live in grace, love in grace, and grow in grace - for it is through His grace that we are made strong, and it is through His grace that our marriages will truly thrive. So may we always remember to extend grace to one another, just as God has extended it to us. And may this be the foundation upon which our marriage stands forevermore. Amen.

The Role of Communication

In any marriage, communication plays a crucial role in building a strong and healthy relationship. It allows couples to express their thoughts, feelings, and needs effectively and helps them understand each other better. However, communication is not just about talking – it also involves active listening and understanding.

Communication in a marriage is more than just conveying information; it is also about creating a deep connection with your partner. It requires honesty, vulnerability, and trust. When couples communicate openly and honestly, they create a safe space for each other to share their deepest thoughts and emotions.

But effective communication doesn't come easy. It takes effort, patience, and practice. Learning how to communicate effectively can improve the quality of your relationship and help you overcome challenges together.

Tips for Effective Communication

1. Practice Active Listening: Pay attention to your partner when they are speaking and try to understand their perspective without interrupting or making assumptions.
2. Use "I" Statements: Instead of accusing or blaming, use "I" statements to express your feelings without putting the other person on the defensive.
3. Don't Avoid Conflict: It's normal for couples to have disagreements, but it's important not to sweep them under the

rug. Address conflicts calmly and respectfully.

4. Show Empathy: Put yourself in your partner's shoes and try to understand their feelings. This will help you respond with compassion and understanding.

5. Practice Regular Check-Ins: Schedule time to talk about your feelings, concerns, and needs with your partner on a regular basis. This can help prevent build-up of resentment or misunderstandings.

6. Be Open to Feedback: Communication is a two-way street, so be open to receiving feedback from your partner and work together to find solutions.

7. Use Non-Verbal Cues: Pay attention to non-verbal cues such as body language, tone of voice, and facial expressions when communicating with your partner. These can often convey more than words alone.

8. Take Breaks When Needed: If a conversation becomes too heated or emotional, it's okay to take a break and come back to it when both parties are calmer.

9. Seek Outside Help: If you are struggling with communication in your relationship, don't be afraid to seek outside help from a therapist or counselor. They can provide tools and techniques for effective communication.

10. Be Patient: Effective communication takes time and effort, so be patient with yourself and your partner as you work towards improving your communication skills together.

Communication is a vital aspect of any relationship, whether it's romantic, familial, or platonic. By following these tips, you can improve the quality of your communication and strengthen your relationships. Remember to always approach conflicts with an open mind, empathy, and a willingness to work together towards finding solutions. Effective communication takes practice, but the benefits are well worth the effort. So keep at it and continue to nurture healthy and positive communication in all of your relationships.

CONCLUSION

In conclusion, effective communication is essential for building and maintaining healthy relationships. By following the tips mentioned above, you can improve your communication skills and strengthen your connections with others. Remember to always communicate calmly and respectfully, be empathetic towards others, regularly check-in with your partner or loved ones, be open to feedback, pay attention to nonverbal cues, take breaks when needed, seek outside help if necessary, and be patient with the process. With effort and practice, you can become a better communicator and foster healthier relationships in all aspects of your life. So keep these tips in mind and continue to prioritize effective communication for fulfilling and harmonious relationships. Whether it's expressing your thoughts and feelings or actively listening to others, effective communication is key to building strong connections and understanding one another on a deeper level. So make an effort to continuously improve your communication skills, and watch as your relationships flourish. Remember, communication is not just about words but also about the intent and understanding behind them. So keep communicating and building stronger bonds with those around you. Good Blessings!, Now go out there, communicate effectively, and nurture your relationships for a happier and more fulfilled life.

So don't be afraid to engage in open and honest communication, as it is the cornerstone of healthy relationships. Remember to always listen actively, speak respectfully, and approach conflicts with empathy and a willingness to work towards resolution. With these tools, you can navigate any communication challenge that comes your way and build stronger connections with others. Communication is a lifelong skill that requires patience, practice, and continuous effort. But the rewards of improved relationships and a happier life are well worth it. So keep working on your communication skills, be open to feedback, and never stop learning and growing as a communicator. Your relationships will thank you for it! Let's continue to prioritize effective communication in our lives and see the positive impact it has on our relationships and overall well-being. Remember, healthy communication leads to healthier relationships, which ultimately leads to a happier life. So let's make communication a top priority in our daily interactions with others. With patience, effort, and continuous improvement, we can all become better communicators and build stronger, more fulfilling relationships. So go forth and communicate effectively - your relationships will thank you for it! Lastly, always remember the power of words and how they can positively or negatively impact those around us. Choose your words carefully, speak with kindness and understanding, and watch as your relationships flourish. And when in doubt, always remember to listen before speaking – it's amazing what we can learn and understand when we truly listen to one another. Thank you for taking the time to read this guide on effective communication. I hope it has provided valuable insight and tools that you can apply in your daily life. Here's to building stronger connections and fostering healthier relationships through effective communication!.

Effective communication is not just about speaking, it also involves active listening. When we listen attentively to others, we show them respect and give them the opportunity to share their thoughts and feelings. This can lead to deeper understanding and better communication in our relationships.

In addition to listening, body language plays a crucial role in effective communication. Nonverbal cues such as facial expressions, gestures, and posture can convey just as much information as words. Being aware of our own body language and being able to read others' can greatly enhance our ability to communicate effectively.

Furthermore, it's important to remember that communication is a two-way street. Both parties involved have a responsibility to actively participate and make an effort to understand one another. This means being open-minded, asking questions for clarification, and acknowledging and respecting each other's perspectives.

In today's fast-paced world, technology has become a common method of communication. While it certainly has its benefits, it can also create barriers in effective communication if not used wisely. It's important to be mindful of the tone and context when communicating through technology, as misunderstandings can easily occur without the use of nonverbal cues.

Lastly, effective communication also involves being able to handle conflicts and disagreements in a healthy manner. This includes using

"I" statements, focusing on the issue at hand instead of attacking the person, and actively listening to each other's perspectives.

In conclusion, effective communication is essential for building strong relationships and fostering understanding. By incorporating active listening, body language awareness, open-mindedness, technology etiquette, and conflict resolution techniques into our daily lives, we can greatly improve our ability to communicate with others. Remember to always strive for clear and respectful communication in all aspects of your life! So keep practicing these skills and watch your relationships flourish. Let's continue to foster a culture of effective communication and understanding.

Understanding also helps us to grow and learn from each other, creating a more inclusive and empathetic society. As individuals, we have the power to make a positive impact through our communication skills. Let's use them wisely and make meaningful connections with those around us. Communication is truly a powerful tool that can bring people together and bridge differences. So let's continue to improve upon it and create stronger bonds in all aspe cts of our lives. Keep communicating effectively, keep understanding, and watch the positive effects ripple out into the world around you! Overall, effective communication is not just about exchanging information, but also building trust, respect, and understanding between individuals. It is a skill that requires practice and effort, but the benefits it brings to our personal and professional lives are invaluable. So let's continue to prioritize effective communication and strive for better connections with others. Remember, communication is key in all relationships, so let's make sure we're using it effectively! Let's also remember to be patient with ourselves and others as we navigate through various forms of communication. With time, effort, and an open mind, we can all become better communicators and create a more harmonious world around us. So Let's strive to create a world where effective communication is cherished and fostered, resulting in stronger relationships and a more harmonious society for everyone. Continue to communicate effectively and seek understanding as we allow God to guide us back to His righteousness.

Made in the USA
Columbia, SC
03 September 2024